Christmas in

Fair Bend

D1553265

Angie Ellington

Purchase additional copies in Kindle
electronic format or in paperback
from www.amazon.com

SERIES: *A MOONLIT HEARTS ROMANCE*

CHRISTMAS IN FAIR BEND

Work of Fiction
This book is a work of fiction. The names, characters, places, and incidents are products of the writer's imagination or have been used fictitiously and are not to be construed as real. Any resemblance to persons, living or dead, actual events, locales or organizations is entirely coincidental. ***Note: There are a few non-fiction references to cities, states, and businesses or locations. (Fair Bend is intended to be a fictional town, along with any businesses included in that area. If an actual Fair Bend, NC exists, I did not find it in research and it would not be the town in my story if it does. I did find an East Bend, NC after writing a portion of the story that coincidentally is within an hour or so from Charlotte, although in a different direction than my vision of Fair Bend. Romelle's is also a fictional retail company).*

E book Edition

Acknowledgments

Thank you for your support. Dedicated to my family and friends.

TABLE OF CONTENTS

Chapter One

Summer-- 10 years ago

"I wanted to tell you last week, but with everything going on with graduation and you leaving early to go back home, I decided to wait until I could tell you face to face." Lacey Myers was trembling with emotions while telling her boyfriend of five years that she had accepted a paid internship with a large retail chain based in Boston. She wasn't sure if it was the right decision, but she knew she'd regret it if she didn't see this through.

"When did you apply for a job in Boston? I thought you were all set to start as a junior designer with Celine's?" (Celine's was an interior design firm based in Charlotte about an hour from their hometown of Fair Bend, North Carolina). "When did this happen? I know things aren't going exactly as planned for us, but I thought we at least still agreed that our future was together." Mason Peters was feeling deflated. Like he had been hit by a truck. He didn't know how to respond to this. A job offer in Boston and a move several states away. This was not what they had planned after college graduation. They had discussed marriage and moving in together after college. That had always been the plan.

Lacey fought back tears. "Everything just happened so quickly. I found out about the position in my final lecture from our T.A. I was only mulling it over to discuss with you when you shared the news of your grandfather's cancer diagnosis and that your dad needed you to move back home to help with the electrical business. We had discussed moving to Charlotte, but not back to Fair Bend." Lacey couldn't stop herself and before she could stop the words, they spilled out abruptly. "Small towns are not going to give either of us the opportunities we need at this stage of our lives and the career goals we have. At least not my career goals. You wanted to be an engineer. Not settle and be an electrician. I—I didn't mean that. Mason, I don't mean to criticize you." She wished she could take that back. It just came out. The guilt and sadness of leaving Mason was overwhelming her, but she had to do what was best for her. She was only 22 years old. She couldn't make her plans based on her boyfriend's choices. She wanted more.

Their lives had been a bubble in college. They had been together since their senior year of high school and friends since they were kids. It was time to take chances that didn't include each other. She wanted to be an interior designer, but that was a long way off. If she worked at Celine's, she wouldn't have the opportunities she could have with a large corporation. Perhaps, becoming an interior designer and owning her own firm may not happen, but she would gain respect and connections in a large market. That's how she would make a name for herself. She needed to prove herself. That would not happen in Fair Bend. She didn't want to resent Mason for being the reason she didn't take this opportunity and truth be told, moving to Charlotte was settling for Lacey. She wanted to experience new things. She needed to find out if there was more for her than getting married after college and working in a mediocre position.

"I'm sorry, Mason. I know you are doing what is best for your family. That's one of the things I love most about you; your commitment to family and ability to take charge when people need you. I just....I'm not ready for the same life that I think you are. Not right now. You'll be happy back home. I won't be. Not if I don't see for myself where this could lead for me." Lacey sighed heavily. She had stood her ground. She had convinced herself she was making the right choice. At least mostly.

"The same life? I thought being together was what you wanted. Moving forward after college together. Supporting each other. I've always supported your dreams. I just can't support you following them so far away; at least not now when I'm committed to helping my family with the business. I guess I just didn't expect you to choose career first. I wouldn't ask you to choose me first either. I...I guess I assumed—hoped... you would at least choose opportunities that could benefit you *with* me...not *without*."

Mason felt his heart sink into his chest and knew by the look on Lacey's face that her mind was made up. He would be wasting his breath to try and convince her to stay. If he had to convince her, it wasn't meant to be. He had to let her go. She was meant for bigger things. Traveling, expensive things, and someone who could provide her with what she wanted to be happy, even if it wasn't what she necessarily needed. He could see Lacey had changed. She wanted different things and he wasn't part of her plans anymore.

"You do what you need to, Lacey. If moving to Boston is what your heart is telling you to do...then it's what you should do. I've never wanted to be the guy who stood in the way of your dreams. I would never make you happy if you stayed. Not now. You're right. You would resent me and so would I because I'd wonder if *we* were...if *I* were enough."

Two weeks later, Lacey moved to Boston. She had second guessed herself enough. She had to find out what she really wanted. Mason was right. They wouldn't have been happy if she had stayed. She had to follow a path of her own. So did he. They stayed in touch for a while, but eventually all communication ended.

Chapter Two

(Present Day) December 1ˢᵗ..................(Dates and days of the week are not sequential with any particular yearly calendar)

Lacey packed frantically for her tenth business trip in six weeks to begin negotiations in completing the final acquisition of the year for the spring home goods line at Romelle's; one of the nation's largest retailers of home décor, housewares, and clothing. She paused when a call coming in reminded her that her mother had already left two voice mails in the last week & was now calling again after her one day pit stop back home over Thanksgiving during a week of back to back meetings. She was barely able to fly home for the day; not even the day. A few hours. She had landed at 9 AM, spent the day with her family in a whirlwind Thanksgiving dinner, and rushed back to the Charlotte airport by 8 that evening to return to Boston before a meeting the next morning with her team.

She had not been able to go home for Christmas the past two years due to her hectic work schedule. Last year had been the worst Christmas ever as her ex-boyfriend, Cooper, was in California for business after promising he was going to get back in time to spend a few days over the holidays with her so she stayed in Boston. It was a good thing she hadn't booked a flight home as she became ill with a nasty sinus infection, and felt miserable the entire week. Cooper kept delaying his flight home and acting shady about why he wasn't coming back. Lacey assumed it was because he was afraid he would have to take care of her versus hanging out in the California sun. She had spent Christmas Day watching old movies on the couch in her flannel pajamas, drinking peppermint tea and snacking on left over Hickory Farms crackers and cheese her roommate had left in the fridge. To top it off, the jerk had called the next day breaking things off over the phone when he was offered a job in L.A. He didn't even bother to do it in person when he returned to Boston prior to relocating.

Lacey had understood that the one thing she had in common above anything else with Cooper was ambition and the mindset that career came first for both of them. Despite being driven and agreeing on all things business related, their relationship was more about appearances such as work dinners and social events; benefits for advancement in careers. She was far from devastated when that relationship ended, but it would've been nice to have someone in her life that cared enough to bring her soup when she didn't feel well and ring in the new year with. Her roommate, Darcy was in England with her parents and her boyfriend. Lacey had told herself she only felt lonely because she was sick. Otherwise, she would've kept busy and never felt those holiday blues.

This year there wouldn't be any time for feeling sorry for herself because she would be alone. She hoped a promotion was on the horizon as she'd been burning the candle at both ends for far too long and the dream position was finally within reach. This was her year. Her time to shine. This was THE DEAL she needed so family would just have to understand if she couldn't be there for another holiday celebration. They would understand. They were used to Lacey not being home for the holidays. She was trying to convince herself they wouldn't be disappointed, although she knew they would be. Hence, the repeated calls from her mother.

She only needed to close this final deal with Alberson's for the spring line that would give Romelle's the monopoly on the trendy new limited home décor line. She just had to get through this meeting with the Alberson project team leader and hopefully landing that final meeting in with the Executive VP of the new line to seal the deal.

As her phone alerted her to yet, another voicemail from her mother, Lacey tossed her heels into her carry-on bag, raced downstairs, grabbed her coat and floppy hat that she had worn on every flight these past six insanely busy weeks as she was of the belief it was bringing her good luck. Besides, being fashionable and promoting clothing from Romelle's was definitely a necessity and the hat was the perfect accessory for those flight selfies when she hash-tagged Romelle's.

The uber driver was waiting by the sidewalk of her apartment building and whisked her to the airport.

"I will have to call mom back when I land and get settled into the hotel room" Lacey thought as she listened to her mom's message reminding her to make time for a visit home for Christmas. The guilt trip had been laid on heavily in the voice mails and it's not that she didn't want to visit, but once again, things were just too busy with work to fit in a visit like her parents wanted. A full week. She hadn't had a week off in almost three years outside of one week in the summer two years ago when she traveled to London with her roommate Darcy for what was supposed to be a vacation. Darcy was British, although she had only lived in England until the age of ten. Her father still resided there, and she would visit annually.

Even that turned into work. Her boss had

called and landed her a rare meeting with an exec from one of their vendors of cookware that wasn't even Lacey's department. Since she was there, she could represent the company for the meeting. Never mind the fact she was on vacation for the first time in a year at that point. Of course she had attended the meeting which turned into a second meeting at the end of the week with video calls back in the states. So much for touring London. She had two days out of seven to actually see any of the city and it had poured rain during one of the only days she got to tour the sights. "So much for meeting the royal family. I'm certain I would have if I had the time" she had scoffed to Darcy.

Chapter Three

"Well, it went fantastic! I feel really good about this meeting. Just one more hurdle with the new VP in a few weeks, although I'm a little worried about his experience level. He's Mr. Alberson's grandson and this is his first major project. I just hope he's focused on the stakes at hand and not just in a position given to him because of his grandfather, " Lacey shared in conversation with Darcy.

Lacey always called Darcy after big meetings as they had been best friends since they worked together at Romelle's when first moving to Boston. They were both interns. Darcy was now working as a marketing manager for a widely known cosmetics brand. They both have done well with their career aspirations thus far, although Darcy had turned down an offer six months earlier to work for a competing cosmetics brand due to the increased travel and commute bi-weekly to Manhattan. It's true she would have lived out of her suitcase even more than Lacey had she accepted the position, but all Lacey could see was the boost in her career that she just let pass her by. What an opportunity for Darcy, but it was her decision. She was not Darcy. She would have jumped at the opportunity.

Darcy made her choice based on other goals. She wanted to get married and start a family. She had been dating her boyfriend for almost two years and she said he'd turned down an offer to relocate to Dallas for her, so she wanted to show the same level of commitment to a future together. Lacey knew Darcy would be moving out soon and she dreaded that day. It wasn't because she didn't want Darcy to be happy, but because it would mean that they would see each other much less and although they had reached their early thirties, both 32 years old, it would be an adjustment not having her around.

Lacey lived for Wine Wednesdays and Chinese takeout nights. With such a busy work schedule, social life was limited. Date nights even when Lacey was with Cooper were rare as he was often out of town when she wasn't. Thankfully, Darcy had been not only an amazing friend, but a great roommate who made time for their friendship even around her own busy schedule and relationship.

The girls gabbed for a few minutes longer when Darcy practically screamed through the phone "I can't wait until you're back; I was going to, but I can't! I'm engaged! Mark proposed tonight at dinner." It was the anniversary of their first date...or the first time they met..or something. Lacey could never keep up with all of the PDA-packed couple's special moments. She couldn't imagine celebrating the first moment she met someone as she tried to remember when she first met Cooper and she couldn't be certain. It was sometime in the summer.

"I'm over the moon excited for you guys." She really was happy for Darcy. "We're getting married in Aruba New Year's Eve and Lace...I will be moving out when we return, but I am going to start moving in with Mark this weekend. I hate to move out over the holidays as we always have fun when we're both home watching Hallmark movies and drinking cheap holiday wines." Darcy was always the planner for their *roomie* nights. She was more into that kind of stuff than Lacey. If Lacey were on her own, she probably would never get around to even decorating a tree. Maybe a wreath would make it to the door of their apartment, but that's about it. She just didn't have the time, nor really the inclination. Maybe if there were someone to celebrate with and if she had more time to spend back home. Well, she had chosen this life. Career now. There's time.

As they ended their conversation, Lacey suddenly felt a sadness take over. She was losing her roommate, although financially, she could handle that. They had continued living together because they got along so well and hadn't let sharing an apartment ruin their friendship as often happens. Now, it would be just a lonely apartment. No roommate, no boyfriend, not even a cat, as the cat she loved belonged to Darcy and would also be leaving her. She couldn't even have a pet because she was away so often for work. She realized she didn't have much of a life of her own. Work was all she had.

She broke her gaze when a commercial for Romelle's came on the hotel television. It was the first day of the run of their holiday promotional campaign for all US markets. She had seen it several times throughout production but watching it on television broke her temporary gloom. "It's just the holidays. I know what my plan is," she said aloud. She decided to take a walk down the street to a nearby coffee shop for an Americano.

She sat at the table by a window in the coffee shop, feeling mixed emotions. She was confident in her meeting, where she was in her life career-wise, and happy for Darcy. "This year is ending on a high note. I'm in Chicago. It's a beautiful Christmas view in this historical shopping center and I'm enjoying my coffee. Life is good."

Still all the while, sadness was there in the back of her mind as she watched couples around her in the coffee shop, walking by the Christmas tree outside, and holding hands while strolling the sidewalks with bags in hand. <u>Jingle Bell Rock</u> started playing in the background. She smiled as this made her think of Fair Bend. Christmases from her childhood flashed through her mind with her late grandparents, her sister, parents, and other family and friends who would gather a few days before Christmas and have a bonfire, drink hot cocoa and roast marshmallows. She had fond memories of holidays growing up in North Carolina.

She never really thought about those moments much anymore as holidays were just days. Christmas was now more about holiday shoppers, sales figures, deadlines, and product placement for Lacey. She had made an effort the first couple of years in Boston to engage in holiday festivities. There was no shortage of spectacular light displays and events to attend. Ice skating at Boston Common was her favorite winter activity with Darcy when they first relocated to the city. Viewing the lighting of the tree and skating was magical. Even Romelle's was a tour stop for tourists and residents alike, with its' whopping five trees located throughout the store and the window displays that were truly works of art. Literally, as they hired artists to design them. Still, Lacey had lost her enchantment with all holidays. Although she would contribute her lack of enthusiasm as a side effect of a rising career, it was more than that.

She didn't get to go home and her family didn't like to travel and wouldn't fly on an airplane, so coming to Boston had never happened. Maybe that was part of why she didn't try harder to plan a trip home for the holidays and why in ten years, she had been home maybe a dozen times and never for more than a few days.

She knew when she moved to Boston that only her older sister Kara, would make the trip to see her, and even that was rare, as she was a stay at home mom in Denver, CO with twin boys at the rambunctious age of seven. She had visited more often when Lacey first moved to Boston, but after her husband, Ted's job transfer to Denver, Kara became pregnant and she may have visited twice since the boys were born.

To be fair, she had tried to plan a visit a few other times; even over the holidays before when Lacey couldn't make it home to Fair Bend, but Lacey had always been too consumed with work to be worth the trip. They would want to visit and tour Boston. Take the kids to the New England Aquarium and the Franklin Park Zoo. If it were summer, get tickets to Fenway. They had done that once when Lacey first moved to Boston.

Maybe she could get home for a visit next Christmas. After the promotion she hoped for had happened, although she didn't envision things slowing down in her schedule if that happened. Well, maybe she should try for a one day visit again like she did for Thanksgiving.

She wouldn't be working Christmas Eve or Christmas Day this year, but she could really use a day to rest during that time. Christmas in Fair Bend is not a time for rest. Not with two seven year old nephews running around and mom and dad arguing over how to cook the turkey..oven roasted or deep fried. Dad and the deep fryer. She laughed at the thought of her last Christmas at home when the fryer had a hole in the bottom that was discovered just as her dad was ready to drop the turkey in it. It was quite the day, but she was thankful for the time to be with them.

She buttoned her coat and tucked her scarf inside as she left the coffee shop. It was starting to snow. A cold front had been predicted with snow accumulation expected in Chicago. She hoped her flight back to Boston would be on time bright and early tomorrow, but for now, she would enjoy breathing in the crisp air and feeling the light damp snowflakes falling around her face on her walk back to her hotel room.

Chapter Four

After arriving at the office around three in the afternoon rather than late morning due to a delayed flight, Lacey was feeling the pressure of the meeting with her boss that had been scheduled that morning via text message. A meeting she had to postpone already due to her flight delay, so she had no time to prepare herself for the review of yesterday's meeting. She had been in two cities in less than 24 hours which was par for the course, but she needed a break.

Her boss, a short balding man with a gray suit on that was ill-fitting burst in the door on his cell phone. She sat in the chair trying not to spin out of nervousness waiting for his call to end. This reminded her of spinning on the stool in her dad's hardware store. He was pacing and pulling his pants up every few seconds that hung below his midsection and exposed his shirt button squeezing open enough to see his Hanes ribbed shirt underneath slightly. Seriously? He works for a company with suits in all sizes. Couldn't he just call down for a bigger shirt and perhaps suspenders would be a good investment, as well. Mr. Tollerson was a brilliant business man, but had zero taste in personal presentation; especially since splitting with his wife last year. He was never a fashion icon of the office, but his fashion issues were getting worse.

"So, Lacey. I'm very impressed with how things are going with Alberson's. Things really are shaping up with this acquisition. You are showing me that you're almost ready for more responsibility. {What does he mean, almost? I've been busting my hump for...} "Lacey? You listening?" "Oh, umm. Yes, Mr. Tollerson. All ears." Lacey had to grit her teeth not to question the *almost* remark. She had hoped he was going to discuss her new role with the company as VP of the home goods division that she had been pitching for quite some time since becoming the lead buyer of the department with the lowest cost to product ratio and highest sales of any department in Romelle's last year. Not to toot her own horn, but toot...toot.

"Lacey, I need you to handle a startup for our Charlotte, North Carolina store. As you know, the store is the first in that state and we are trying to gain a presence in the south. We are hitting all of our targets in the northeast, mid-west, and now, I'm hoping to secure a store in each state from Virginia to Florida in the largest market in each state. We have done well with our launch in Chesapeake, Virginia. Now, we need to hit the ground running in

Charlotte.

I've had several others involved and I know this doesn't fall under your job description, but you are familiar with the area and the demographics. I think you would be an asset in overseeing inventory displays and making sure as our senior home goods buyer that the window displays will get people in the door."

Mr. Tollerson leaned forward in his seat and crunched his hands into a fist. His coffee spattered a little when he pressed down on the table. Lacey was drifting. Why was she so distracted? "So, can I count on you Lacey?" She paused still slightly in a daze. "Yes, yes sir. Umm. Sure. Mr. Tollerson. I can handle any task. I'm up for the challenge." Lacey felt herself starting to oversell. "When exactly did you need me to be in Charlotte?" "Day after tomorrow. Call down and have the travel department handle the details. You can stay with your family, right? It would save the company money which makes you even more valuable. Aren't they close by?" Typical. Always trying to save a buck.

If it were anyone else in the company, he'd have to pay for accommodations, but that's why he selected Lacey. She knew that. A way to penny-pinch. She would do it. She needed to stay in his good graces and let's face it. Saying no wasn't really an option anyway. It would give her mother great pleasure knowing her long lost daughter would be home for a few weeks during the holidays. That hadn't happened since college. Darcy would be moving out gradually through the holidays anyway and this way, it would feel more like ripping off the band-aid than feeling the full sadness of her friend moving out and getting married.

After the meeting, Lacey stopped by her favorite coffee shop to meet Darcy. The Bean Town Beanery was the best. However, after three cups of coffee already today, she switched to hibiscus and cranberry tea. A special brew for the holidays and although Lacey usually avoided specialty drinks, she was feeling a bit of Christmas spirit in the thought of going home for a few weeks. The family Christmas tree was already decorated as her mom always did that Thanksgiving weekend. There used to be a second tree in the foyer that was always decorated by the women. A tradition that had started when she and her sister were in middle school. The sparkle tree. Filled with pink, blue, purple, and silver ornaments. Since she and Kara had moved away, her mom had eventually stopped putting it out.

Lacey sipped her tea and started to reminisce of holidays at home. Something she hadn't done the last few years. Work would still be her first priority as she was there to do a job and she would do it well. However, a little time for family and visiting some of the old shops in

Fair Bend would be nice. She was always in and out of town so quickly that she rarely saw anyone outside of her immediate family while there. She hadn't kept in touch with people from high school during college much. Only a few and over the years, those friendships had dissipated. She followed people on social media, but she wasn't really into that. She mainly used social media to look up information related to work. She hadn't even logged in to any of those accounts in months.

She leaned in and smelled the combination of tart and sweetness of her tea. After taking a sip, she picked up her phone. "Hi, mom. Yes, I know. I've been meaning to call you back. Mom...mom...hello. Can I just... Veronica Myers continued to rant about why Lacey hadn't made time to return her phone call. Lacey started rolling her green eyes and then smiled. "Mom, I'm coming home. I'll be home for Christmas. Well, sort of. I'll explain when I see you in two days. I've got to go. Darcy's walking in to meet me. Yes, it's true." Her mom was bellowing with glee in the background to Lacey's father. "Our baby's spending Christmas with us this year. The whole family will be here." Veronica was rejoicing and Lacey felt she was listening to a preaching service. "Praise the Lord, praise the Lord my children will be home for Christmas" as Lacey heard dishes rattling. Her mom was always multitasking. "OK, I've gotta go. Love you too." Lacey couldn't resist giggling at her mother's joy.

I'll Be Home for Christmas started playing in the coffee shop and Lacey smiled and sipped her holiday inspired tea. Why didn't she order this every year perhaps a few times she was thinking as she warmed her hands around her cup. Usually she'd only try it once to appease Darcy and then back the standard Americano. This year she would try to be more open to the holiday offerings while visiting back home. It would help with the store layout by being more in the holiday spirit; provide inspiration. Either way, she was enjoying switching up from her normal routine. Christmas tea instead of coffee...spending December in North Carolina rather than traveling all over the country. A definite change from her routine.

Chapter Five

Darcy bounced in, two velvet cupcakes in a red box in hand from the bakery next door. Yes, Bean Town Beanery sold baked goods, but not cupcakes. The owner of the cupcake shop next door made them homemade daily and didn't even open until noon. It was such a teaser and actually a great marketing tactic to have people walking by in the mornings to get their cup of joe and smell chocolate, cinnamon, and all other kinds of gooey goodness baking, knowing they would have to wait. The owners of the coffee shop weren't fans, but didn't prohibit bringing them in as long as you were patrons of their products, as well. Lacey shook her head as Darcy giggled. "What? Who would dare eat a cupcake without a cup of coffee anyway? I mean, that would just be wrong, Darcy said swinging her coat around her chair and unwrapping her wool scarf. "Not us. That is for sure. That would be like eating pasta without drinking a glass of Cabernet. That's just not normal," Lacey added.

"So, what's the big news you texted me about?" inquired Darcy. "Mr. Tollerson appointed me to oversee the opening of Romelle's...in Charlotte." "Charlotte? So, you'll be going home for this? How long will you get to be there?" "A few weeks. I will drive down day after tomorrow." "You're not flying?" "No. He wants me to stay for a few weeks, so I'm going to stay with my parents in Fair Bend. It was Mr. Tollerson's strong suggestion, but I likely would have done it anyway. It makes sense. I did make the company spring for a rental rather than driving my own SUV. I'd like to keep the mileage off since it's only a lease and I am finishing the lease in January. I'm too close to going over the mileage allowance so a drive to NC and driving back and forth to Charlotte a few days per week definitely would put me over." "For sure. You need to drive the most expensive car they have just to stick it to Tollerson for making you sweat over this promotion" Darcy scoffed as she took a bite of her cupcake. "True, but I'm so close to getting everything I've been working so hard for. I'm just going to roll with the punches."

"Lacey, you've got this. The promotion is in the bag, I'm sure of it. My concern is if it will make you happy. You moved here wanting to work for Romelle's as a buyer basically to bide your time and eventually become a designer. You had hoped you'd start a line and they would sign you on for the home goods department. You are truly talented and I hope that old bugger Mr. Tollerson, realizes how valuable you are.

I know you have the cutest pillows, throws, and duvets in our apartment and you recovered the old couch and chair we got for free from the neighbors a few years back and made them look fabulous! You've worked really hard for Romelle's. I just hope they give you what you deserve." Darcy would always say what she meant and meant what she said. She was right. Lacey was caught up in titles and monetary rewards these days and had put her interior design dream more on the back burner as a someday goal that may never happen.

"I know. I will continue to design and create. I just may not get to do it professionally. At least, not any time soon. Someday, though. Dreams change with reality as you hit your thirties. At least for me, it seems like my career is heading in a different direction. I still have the apartment to continue sprucing and of course, Mark's place could use a woman's touch so you can certainly count on me to help you redecorate if you want any help."

"Well, if you're happy, I'm happy for you," Darcy shifted the subject to keep from bringing down the mood. She just wanted Lacey to know she was her cheerleader always. "Let's celebrate successes on the horizon." They cheered by tapping cupcakes and then tea in their takeout cups.

Later that evening, they were discussing Darcy's wedding plans that unfortunately Lacey wouldn't get to be a part of. Darcy's destination wedding, honestly worked out well with everything going on for Lacey even though she would've done whatever necessary to be a part of her best friend's special day if asked.

They decided on a girls' night to celebrate before Lacey headed to North Carolina. They only had the next night available before Lacey would leave, so they planned on attending their favorite local venue for a wine and cheese sampling. It was something they had usually done for birthdays. They were simple in their party lives. The days of staying out dancing until 2 AM were mostly behind them.

They were happier getting dressed up in cocktail dresses and doing a wine and cheese event and listening to jazz for celebrations. Since Darcy was getting married, they would add dancing until maybe midnight at a low key bar with the late twenties and thirties crowd and then they would get an uber home. They felt like they were from a different era. Neither had ever been much into the party scene. They truly were ideal roommates. They even nicknamed each other characters from their favorite TV series--Friends. Darcy was Rachel and Lacey was Monica. Both had Phoebe moments, but Darcy was definitely more easy breezy about balancing work and personal life, whereas Lacey was more OCD about just about every aspect of her life.

That night, Lacey and Darcy stayed up binge watching Hallmark Christmas movies since they would miss out on that tradition this year. Lacey was always making fun of the sappy stories and chiming in with how none of those scenarios played out in reality. Darcy would rebuke her remarks with commentary about having an open mind and heart. They weren't about the level of realistic events in each one, but the possibility of love and happiness if you put yourself out there. Something Darcy was much better at than Lacey. Lacey hadn't believed in fairy tales in a long time. She left those rainbows and butterfly notions of love in Fair Bend when she chose career over the sugar-coated dream of finding her true love at seventeen years of age.

Chapter Six

The next night the ladies celebrated. Sparkles and lace abound. "Darcy, the driver is here." Lacey was waiting for her roommate, who always took longer to get ready, in a deep purple off-the-shoulder velvet mini dress with her sleek black shoulder length hair brushing her collarbone. Black closed toe heels with small glittery silver bows on the top and black hosiery. She hadn't dressed up for a night out outside of work in a few months. Since her birthday most likely. She had a long bob and really had been blessed with shiny thick hair. Both ladies looked stunning.

"Coming, love. Just putting in my earrings." Moments later, Darcy bounced in the living room still trying to get her shoes on. She dazzled in a dark green crop top and a floral pouf skirt that hit just above the knee. Her red hair was twisted into a messy bun and she wore strapped heels with a summer vibe even though it was around 30 degrees out. She wrapped in a faux fur knee length coat and Lacey grabbed her new white knee length wool coat she had just purchased that day from Romelle's to take on her business trip to North Carolina. They took a selfie before heading out the door of their quaint apartment in the Brighton area of Boston.

The bartender at their favorite wine bar promptly brought over a wine flight on a metal tray with a cheese sampler of brie, gouda, and gorgonzola with crackers. Each of them had a sampler of five wines in small glasses. The table was festive. Gold and silver linen tablecloths, mistletoe at both entrances, and small flickering battery-operated wax candles adorned each table. Rose gold lights were strung along the bar area and Christmas instrumental jazz provided an ideal setting for a fun, yet low-key evening celebrating Darcy's engagement and upcoming holiday nuptials.

Upon leaving the wine bar, Lacey and Darcy danced to hip-hop and pop music reminiscing of their nights out when they first became friends. They could still shake their booties like they did then, but their elation for doing so didn't last as long now as it had in their mid twenties.

 They may have been home and eating ice cream by midnight, but they had spent a few hours being carefree and Lacey needed that.

As Lacey lie in bed that night, she envisioned what it must be like to have both love and career. To not have to make a choice. She found herself thinking back ten years earlier when she chose career over love. Although she knew it was the right decision at the time, she did wonder on occasion how Mason was doing. He wasn't on social media and she made it a point with her family years ago not to talk about him. She knew he had been married for a while, but wasn't any longer. She knew he still lived in Fair Bend, but that's about all. If his name did get mentioned, she hastily changed the subject. She didn't want to know. It was best to leave the past in the past. What's the saying? Don't look back. You're not going that way...or something profoundly corny like that.

As always, when the rare thought of Mason and her past crept into her mind, she quickly shifted thoughts. She would think of Darcy's happy news. She found herself drifting back. Why couldn't she shake thinking back to someone she said goodbye to a decade ago? She was sure he didn't waste any time thinking of her.

She had so many things going on and great people in her life. There was no need to go down memory lane tonight just because she would spend the next few weeks in Fair Bend. If she ran into Mason, she would be polite and catch up, but too much time had passed. There wouldn't be any awkwardness now. Not after all this time.

Chapter Seven

December 4ᵗʰ......

"I'm on I-85. I'll be there in about an hour. I'm just outside of Charlotte." Lacey was talking with her mother through the Bluetooth in her rental Lexus, which was the same model as her leased Lexus; just a different color. She wanted to drive a vehicle she was comfortable in and knew her way around in for the long drive down to North Carolina.

She had listened to every genre on the radio except for Christmas thus far. She was warming to the idea of the holidays this year, but she knew it would be all that would be playing at Romelle's. The store had just opened a week before Thanksgiving. She was going to be in for quite the challenge helping oversee the first full month's launch during the busiest shopping month of the year. She contemplated stopping by the store on her way to Fair Bend, but it was already 7Pm. She was tiring of the drive and ready to get some much needed rest. She would have the weekend to spend relaxing with her family and that was a welcomed change of pace.

"I've made your favorite. Lasagna and salad. I got the whole wheat noodles. I know you prefer those." Veronica Myers was nothing if not attentive to her family's every need. She loved spoiling her girls and the grandchildren when they were home and would take pride in planning meals based on Lacey and Kara's childhood favorites. "Sounds delicious. I am starving! I haven't eaten since a stop in Maryland. That was a Kind bar and a Greek yogurt from a convenience mart. I'm seriously running on caffeine only at this point and that's fading fast. I'll see you soon." Lacey was ready to get this long drive behind her. She understood why her parents didn't want to make the drive to Boston by car. She didn't like to drive more than two or three hours anywhere herself and rarely did. She was usually racking up frequent flier miles and catching cabs basically everywhere she went. Long road trips were no fun alone for sure.

As she took the exit to Fair Bend, Lacey decided to give the Christmas music a chance for the last few minutes of her journey to her hometown. She started singing along to the radio as she recalled memories from different places along the route. Her childhood best friend's home. She was now living in Wilmington. The spot where her friends would hang out in a parking lot by the old grocery store that had closed down a few years ago and was still for sale. A vacant lot that a new group of teenagers were utilizing. She hoped they weren't getting into trouble. Then again, she knew people had hoped the same of her group of friends.

She pulled into the long driveway to her parents' home in a wooded lot with a farm next to it. They didn't own it, but she had many fond memories of her neighbors who didn't have children teaching she and Kara to ride horses. Her dad would fish with Mr. Willis and her mom would gossip with Mrs. Willis. They still lived next door. They still had horses and ran a small equestrian school. Her mom kept her informed of everyone in town. Well, everyone except....she was home. She broke her train of thought and started getting her bags. Her dad came out to help. "Welcome home, my love. We've got you here for a few weeks is what your mom said. Is that right?"

"Yes, daddy. I'm here until after Christmas. I will be working a lot in Charlotte while I'm in town. I'm overseeing the new store that recently opened." "Well, let's see if we can turn a few weeks into a much longer stay. We'll feed ya and you can come by the hardware store and we'll have coffee. You'll see what you've been missing from the big city. Peace and quiet. Fresh country air. You won't want to go back to all of that traffic and noise." Rick Myers hadn't lost a thing outside of Fair Bend as he would say. He was content with simple pleasures of life. Fishing, a little hunting (mostly just talking-they never actually would shoot anything), and grilling in his backyard.

He had owned the hardware store on Main St. for over twenty years. He had bought it when the former owner had passed away and his wife was going to have to close down. He had worked for him as a teenager before working swing shifts at a local rubber plant. He always was tinkering and using every tool imaginable, so when the hardware store became available, it was meant for him to take it over.

"Come on in the house. The wind is starting to pick up. It's been mild here for the past couple of days, but a cold front is on the way." "I read that. I think it's following me. It was snowing in Chicago at the earlier part of the week on my trip and was supposed to start tonight in Boston."

That evening, Lacey talked with her parents about work and her promotion she was hoping to get any day now. They had dinner and Lacey fell asleep on the couch while her dad watched an old Clint Eastwood movie and her mom read a romance novel. It felt like old times growing up in her childhood home. Lacey was asleep in her pajamas before 10 PM. Her mother brought in a pillow and an extra blanket and put on her daughter. She wouldn't bother to wake her. Their daughter was home. Even if it was just for a few weeks, she was there. They all slept well that night.

Chapter Eight

"Lacey, let's go!" Veronica bellowed up the stairs. "Be right down. Just have to get this email sent." Even though it was Saturday, Lacey had been on the road all day Friday and hadn't been able to correspond to any of her messages so that morning, she hadn't joined her parents for breakfast much to their dismay. She had grabbed a blueberry muffin (her mom made the best ones she had ever had), a large cup of coffee and headed back upstairs to get on her laptop. She had kissed her mother on the cheek as she took a bite of the muffin and winked at her dad, who shook his head at his force-to-be-reckoned-with of a daughter. "Be sure you're ready by noon to go into town with me to pick up some things and we'll have lunch at Parker's." Veronica was making plans already.

Lacey came down the stairs. "Mom, it's my first day home. We do have some time, ya know." Lacey was rolling her eyes as she looked for her purse. As Veronica stood in the hallway holding Lacey's purse, she smirked; " Well, we're only used to having you here for about 24 hours or less, so it's ingrained in me to fill our days." "Yes, mother dear" Lacey laughed as she rounded the corner and saw Veronica smiling and dangling the bag.

41

Lacey and Veronica were enjoying their mother/daughter day shopping in The Bend, the local town shopping area designed in a village style marketplace. Fair Bend was a quaint little town with a few eclectic shops and the standard fan-fare of businesses. Lacey had always appreciated that most of the citizens shopped locally for most things. If they could get it in Fair Bend, why would they go anywhere else? That was the mentality and it had helped keep businesses in the area thriving while many small town businesses were going under elsewhere. They had lunch at Parker's Diner, which had been a staple to Fair Bend for almost fifty years. It was family owned and had been passed down, as several businesses in the area were. Lacey would imagine having her own design firm in The Bend one day as a teenager, but by the time she left for college, she had forgotten that idea. She felt she needed a large market to be successful at anything in her plans.

After several people said their hellos to Lacey and Veronica, Lacey snickered. "That's small town life for ya. Everyone knows your name. It's like Cheers." Veronica retorted "I know you think that is annoying, but there are certainly times when you would be thankful for the kindness and generosity that comes with 'everyone knowing your name'. "And your business" Lacey scoffed. "Speaking of people who like to know your bus--"Lacey was interrupted by the snobbiest girl from her teenage years. The insufferable Alexia Dodson. Actually, according to social media, it's now Alexia Dodson-Renoir. "Lacey Myers. How *are* you? It's been ages. High school days, I guess." The high-pitched voice was the same screeching nails-on-a-chalkboard sound as ever. "I'm great, Alexia. How are you?" Lacey really didn't care.

As a matter of fact, Alexia was one of the reasons she avoided social media. She detested constantly seeing posts about her car, her boat, her fancy house that seriously looked like it belonged on a celebrity tour of homes, and her constant bragging about their vacations and new this and that. Every time something new was the trendy thing to have, Alexia seemed to post about having it. She had married a man much older and very wealthy. Not surprising, as she was the epitome of fit and beauty. It was apparent she spray tanned, kept her hair appointments on a strict schedule as to not let even the start of roots begin to show, and had on makeup that looked as though it had been professionally applied.

Lacey was a bit in awe of this magazine-worthy look if she were honest with herself, as she sat there with her hair in a ponytail, Lululemon leggings and a "But First Coffee" sweatshirt on with only foundation and lip gloss.

"I'm fabulous, of course. Busy as a bumblebee

all the time with my fit from home business for busy mothers. (Lacey was remembering now some posts last year about that. She was trying to get people to pay her for tips on how to work out on furniture and the dryer or something). "I'm just in town to drop off Brinkley-Baxter (is that her son or her dog?) and then on my way to run a few errands for my husband who's working in Palm Springs at the moment. He's a cardiologist, you know? Of course, you know. You are on my facebook page. I'm sure you keep up with all of my events. I'm still hoping you will join one of my courses for fitness from home soon. I guarantee you'll be more toned in just a few weeks." Lacey couldn't stop herself from tilting her head to the side and rubbing her tongue in her cheek while squinting. It was her tell-tale sign of annoyance.

"Actually, I'm never on social media. Too busy with work. Busy bumblebee over here too." She couldn't resist sounding overly perky. "Good to see you. Gotta get going." Thankfully, the check had arrived and Lacey had an excuse to cut the conversation short. After Alexia went over to the counter for her chicken salad sandwich, which Lacey overheard her say was for Brinkley-Baxter who was in the car with her mother and something about it not being for her as she wouldn't dare eat bread, Lacey looked at her facebook page while walking out towards the fountain. "Brinkley-Baxter. Son. Not dog."

"You know, things aren't always as they appear. I have heard rumors, but you know I've never been one for gossip. I'll just say that maybe there are reasons why Alexia feels the need to boast about her life. Perhaps she doesn't have the perfect life she describes. No one ever does." Veronica Myers was always the voice of reason and one to flip the coin to see what was on the other side. "She has always been that way. I know she's insecure about her own life. That's why she gloats all the time. It doesn't really phase me," Lacey interjected.

They walked over to the shopping center's common area to one of the park benches. There were a few placed around the fountain that had been built when Lacey was in high school. She remembered tossing pennies in the fountain for good luck. The town council would drain the fountain annually and donate the coins to a local charity after having them rolled and deposited. It was a celebrated event each summer. Lacey took in the view around her. The town's Christmas tree was really quite lovely. The fountain had multicolored light covers over the lights that were secured inside the concrete. She would have to come back at night to see the light show. Although Fair Bend's holiday décor certainly wouldn't compare to Christmas in Boston, which was really magical, it was still special. Simple and timeless as Lacey knew the personal touches of local citizens that went into decorating The Bend and on Main Street, as well. Wreaths adorned each shop door and along Main Street's light posts. Red bows were tied around the tops of the posts with garland wrapped from top to bottom. Each shop in the shopping center had wintry window displays that were all different and represented various holiday themes. Snowflakes and snowmen were in a craft store; A manger scene was in the flower shop. Candy canes and Santa's workshop were in the wine and cheese shop. Her dad's hardware store just down the street on Main had a Charlie Brown Christmas set. There were also representations of other celebrated holidays and everyone in town loved to view them all. Peace on Earth in large wooden cutouts were placed beside the center's tree. Lacey's favorite decoration was still the large Merry Christmas metal display that was attached to the overhang at the entryway of the center. Happy Holidays was on the back exit overhang, as well.

Lacey had spaced out a bit reminiscing about the times she had spent here growing up. Thankful to see the shops still being rented out even if a few of the businesses had changed.

"Lacey? Lace?" A voice she hadn't heard in a decade was calling her name. She looked up from the bench breaking her gaze at the fountain to see Mason Peters standing next to where she sat looking down at her. Six feet tall. Sandy brown hair. Blue eyes. Olive skin. How was it possible he was just as good looking, if not even more so. He was wearing a baseball cap and a button down flannel shirt with a gray t-shirt underneath that was visible by the three buttons he had kept undone. Dark jeans. Not the skinny jean trend she was seeing all over Boston that she and Darcy still just didn't understand. {Why would a man want to wear tight jeans.} Some type of brown work boots. A little scruff around his face, but nothing too visible. He was smiling with the same crooked smile she had admired so many times in her past.

"Mason. Hey." She stood up. {Do we hug? Shake hands-no-or just stand here?} Lacey wondered as she faced the man she had left behind. He kept his hand in his pocket and held a bag in the other hand. "Christmas shopping?" Lacey said quickly trying to avoid an awkward pause. "Birthday. Mom's is tomorrow and I had her something made at the craft store." Mason said casually looking down towards the bag. "That's sweet and very thoughtful." Lacey was hoping she didn't sound too surprised. That didn't seem like something Mason would do. He wasn't much for surprises. He was more traditional with gifts.

Then, again, he was a broke high school then college kid as was she during their courtship and their gifts were always simple. "She told me what she wanted," he laughingly shared. "It really wasn't my idea. I'm doing good to remember to get a gift, but shopping for them has never been my strength. I have to be given a list or hints or something. What about you? I see the bags there. Are you home for the weekend? Celebrating Christmas early or something? From what I hear, you don't ever spend more than a day or two in town. Work must be good." He started looking away avoiding eye contact. "True. I'm rarely ever home, but I'm actually here for a few weeks. I'll be mostly in Charlotte spearheading our new store opening.

I still work for Romelle's and we've opened a store there. We're taking on the South now." Lacey blushed a bit with embarrassment at that remark. "Yes, work is good. Keeps me busy. You know, traveling all the time. I'm up for a promotion to a VP position, so..."She felt like she was sounding a bit like Alexia. "How are you?" How's the business?" Lacey knew little about Mason's life these days, but she did know he was running his family's electrical business. "I'm good. Business is steady. Keeping busy. It's good to see you Lace. I'm glad things are going so well for you." He was looking at Lacey again, but she wished he was still looking away. She hoped there wouldn't be any awkwardness. There was.

"Good to see you too, and happy early birthday to your mom. Tell your parents hello for me won't ya?" She pepped up and smiled in hopes of easing the tension she knew they were both feeling seeing each other after so many years.

"If you're in town for a few weeks, I'm sure I'll run into ya again at some point. I should get going." Mason paused and then turned and walked away. As he walked away, she couldn't avoid watching him. She had broken his heart. She knew it. Surely, he was over it. He had to be. This was just that one strange encounter. If they ran into each other again while she was home, it would be much easier. He looked back and caught her stare. She hurriedly turned and started grabbing her shopping bags. "Nope, that wasn't awkward whatsoever," Lacey muttered as her mother came walking back over to help her with the bags.

"I saw you talking to Mason. Less than 24 hours home and you run into him." Veronica had always adored Mason and although she supported Lacey's dreams, she was sad when their relationship had ended. "Stop, mom. Let's go." Lacey shook her head as Veronica gave a sly grin.

Chapter Nine

December 12th.........

Lacey had spent the first full week in Fair Bend working more than she had expected at Romelle's. There was much to be done and staff meetings had run long each day. She felt a bit overwhelmed although she was making progress. She had been in Charlotte every day and gotten to her parents' home late most evenings. She hadn't had dinner with them but once all week. They were being so gracious about her schedule and were happy she was home, even if they were spending little time with her.

It was finally the weekend and Lacey had promised to have lunch with her mom and and stop by the hardware store to see her dad. Saturday started out better than last weekend. No emails to return or work to do. Lacey had stayed in Charlotte overnight Thursday just to be sure and give undivided attention to work so that she could have some down time over the weekend. She was hoping to only spend a few hours two or three days the next week on site and hoping by the week of Christmas to have everything running smoothly.

Lacey completed a few errands around town before meeting up with Veronica for lunch. Next up, was a stop at the hardware store to see her father. She spent about a half hour watching in awe as her dad interacted with customers. He was always so enthusiastic about helping people find what they needed and knew the perfect tools to suggest for just about every home project anyone was taking on. Having worked there in his younger days and then becoming the owner later on was something he was very proud of and wanted to do justice to the store's success after taking over Mr. Harper's legacy in the community. Mission accomplished. Lacey could see just how much Rick Myers was respected and appreciated. She beamed with pride.

She sat on the stool in the storage room that she would spin on during her childhood. He would always warn her to stop before falling, which she would never do, and of course, eventually she did fall off and fractured her wrist when she landed on it. She did a single spin and when she came around to stop, someone was ringing the bell at the counter watching her through the open door. It was Mason.

She stumbled getting off of the stool before regaining her composure. "First time walking?" Mason joked. "Ha. Ha. Very funny."

Lacey rebuked. "If you're not careful, you'll end up back at the ER. Didn't you break your wrist or hand or something doing that?" Mason retorted. "It was my wrist. A fracture. Good memory. We must have been around twelve," Lacey replied. "We've known each other a very long time. There are lots of memories aren't there?" Mason said, leaning against the door. Lacey was standing in front of Mason by now. " I just need to pick up something your dad has for me in the back." Oh, OK. I'll—I'll go get him." Lacey's dad walked up with the bag. "Hey, Mason. Will you come in the back for a second and check my circuit breaker. I think I've got a short fuse somewhere," Rick said as he processed the order. Mason and Lacey continued exchanging glances at one another. "Sure. I'll take a look." The two men walked to the back of the store.

When they came back to the storefront, Mason stopped at the door and turned around. Lacey didn't know whether to continue the conversation so she leaned over the counter pretending to do something on her phone as he had walked past. "Do you wanna get a cup of coffee or something? Maybe catch up for more than two seconds." After a moment of hesitation, Lacey replied "Yeah, umm. OK. I'll meet you at Java House. Do you mean now..or...?" Lacey didn't want to sound eager. "Now works for me. See you in ten."

Lacey and Mason sat in the back table near the

electric fireplace that was set up as a reading area with newspapers, books people would leave, and magazines. Lacey noticed the newspapers that she rarely saw anymore. She was happy to see printed news and paper books still being looked at more than phones and tablets. There was WiFi, but she noticed an even mix of people using technology and printed reading among the patrons. While she was observing the artwork from a local school on the walls, Mason took her coat and offered to get their beverages.

"Thanks" Lacey said as he sat down across from her with peppermint hot cocoa for her, as she was continuing to try and stick with her vow to be more festive this holiday. Lacey watched Mason hang their coats by the wall-something she would never do anywhere else. He stepped back to allow an elderly lady to pass and held the door for her as she exited. The guys she was used to going out with when she rarely did so would have expected her to pay for her own coffee, and wouldn't have made any gesture to hold the door open or take her coat. Times and people were changing and she was glad Mason had not. This wasn't a date, and he had reasons to avoid her completely, yet here he was, being the perfect southern gentleman.

He had coffee with hazelnut. She recalled that was the way he preferred his coffee in college. No milk. No additional sugar. Just a simple sweetness to an already perfect blend. Kind of like he was. Always just the right balance of sweet and strong-willed. "So, how has your first week back home been? You ready to pack up and head back up north yet? I know quiet nights at home around Fair Bend isn't your scene. You probably paint the town red every chance you get." Mason was doing his usual dance around commentary to ask if she was happy in Boston. "You'd be surprised how similar my nights are in Boston to my nights here in Fair Bend. Just because I live in a big city doesn't mean I live the party lifestyle. I'm really still a low-key kind of girl. It's been different being home being in my old house and spending time with my parents, but in a good way. I've spent most of the week in Charlotte at the store, so I haven't had much down time. Truthfully, I don't get much down time in Boston, either. Work is pretty crazy right now," Lacey replied and then sipped her cocoa.

"You mentioned you're up for a promotion. Will you be designing a line for the company? I know that's what you've always wanted" Mason probed curious if her career dreams she had left him for were coming to fruition. "Yes, hopefully, if I get it. Fingers crossed that this is the last project before that happens," Lacey said in an attempt to reassure herself more than Mason.

Mason shifted the conversation. "And...how's

your personal life going? Anyone special? I would have heard if you were married, I guess." Lacey looked around the room for a moment and then back to Mason. "Umm. There have been people in my life, but no one special right now. I'm too busy to focus much energy on dating and relationships. I date, though. I mean, I do go out. Just not anything serious...right now." She wanted to be clear he understood she could date...if she wanted to. That her personal life was on hold by choice. Mason nodded his head with a half smile. His piercing pale blue eyes lit up a bit with the slight wrinkling of his forehead. Lacey knew the smug look all too well. It was one of his most annoying and yet, most attractive qualities.

She quickly added "So, what about you? Anyone special?" "Yep, sure is." Mason said without hesitation. Lacey was surprised at feeling her heart sink a bit. He paused. Lacey started twitching her mouth and placing a finger slightly in her teeth, which Mason knew was something she did when she was uncomfortable and unsure of how to respond. He then added "My dog, Zeke." They both laughed. "Like you, I...date, but there's no one in particular that I spend much time with.

I was married for a while. I'm sure you heard. But, we wanted different things. She wanted me to move with her when she was offered the opportunity to be groomed to take over a large company in Tampa that her family owned. She had moved here to live with her grandparents when she was in college in Boone and we met through work. I had to work on a business there that she was working for. Anyway, long story short..we met about a year after you...well, after you left. We dated for about a year and she pushed to get married. I wasn't in the best place, but I thought maybe that would help me..well, move on from some things. We thought we were in love, but I think she just wanted to make her parents mad by marrying someone in North Carolina and not moving back to work for her father. She was spoiled and was never satisfied with the lifestyle we lived.

Anyway, we tried, but after about two years, she decided she missed the sunshine state. She wanted me to move there and work for her and her father. Of course, I said no. She knew my life was here when we got married. So, she left. I should have been sad and angry and whatever, but I wasn't. Honestly, I was more relieved. That's really it for relationships since. I date occasionally, but I haven't been in a relationship since then and I've been OK with that. Like you said. It's been my choice to be single. If it's not the real deal, why invest the time? You know early on if the person's worth your effort. I guess I just haven't met anyone in a long time who was really worth my effort."

Lacey felt exactly the same. She could have

made more of an effort with Cooper, but she was relieved when he got the offer to move to L.A. She had told herself at the time she was sad and she wanted to feel angry towards him for not asking her to move with him, even though she knew she wouldn't have. She wasn't mad when she and Cooper broke off their relationship. She was glad she didn't have to invest her efforts in forcing a relationship to work.

Ending her relationship with Mason had been another story. She didn't allow herself to be sad because she didn't want to change her mind. She could tell from this conversation she had hurt him pretty deeply when she left, but he seemed content. He just said he was single by choice.

As they sat and talked about a myriad of topics, time seemed to pass quickly. Mason looked at his watch (he's one to still wear and use his watch rather than looking at a smartphone), and realized over an hour had passed by. Conversation was always easy between them. "What time is it?" Lacey inquired. "Almost 4."

"Wow. I need to get going. I didn't realize we had been here that long. I'm taking my parents out to dinner tonight. They wanted to go around 6 because mom wants me to watch a movie on Hallmark with her at 9. Big night of partying ahead for me as you can see," Lacey chuckled. "Sounds like it. Do you need to make a liquor store run for that movie first?" Mason kidded. "You're joking, but I am actually going to go by The Cellar next door and pick up a couple of bottles of wine."

As they walked out of the coffee shop, Mason reached over and softly removed Lacey's hair from her scarf. "Sorry, I..I just noticed your hair was caught under your scarf and I know you used to hate when that happened." Mason put his coat on and put his hands in his pockets. Lacey stepped in closer. "Thank you. You're right. I do still get irritated by that. This was nice, Mason. I'm glad we can do this. Talk. Hang out and it not be weird. Well, not too weird."

"Yeah, not too weird. It's been ten years. No need to hold on to grudges. I mean, you needed to spread your wings or whatever the saying is. I'm good, Lace. I can tell by the look on your face each time you've seen me that it's like you feel sorry for me. For hurting me. I'm over it. I've been over it for a long time. I understood why you left. Like I said back then, you would've resented me if you hadn't taken that internship and I didn't want to hold you back. I couldn't expect you to stay any more than you could expect me to go if you asked me even now. People have to do what makes them happy and sometimes that means leaving to find out what makes someone happy.

By the way, you still look incredible. I wish you

didn't, so it would make it easier seeing you," he said only partially joking. "Look. No pressure. Just two friends hanging out, but if you aren't busy tomorrow night, a customer gave me tickets to see A Christmas Carol in Charlotte and I wasn't even going to go...I was going to give the tickets to my parents but they have something at church that mom is part of. I hate to waste them but I don't want to go alone either. No big deal. Only if you're not doing anything; would do you care to go with me?" Mason nervously asked.

Mason was rarely bashful about anything. The only time Lacey could recall him stumbling over asking her anything was on their first date that was an actual date instead of hanging out with friends as they usually did. "Sure. I'd love to go. Sounds fun. I haven't had the chance to see a Christmas production in Boston in about three years. My friend Darcy, and I used to go every year to see a show. I've been saying I want to embrace more holiday activities this year since I'm in Fair Bend." Lacey felt a warm tingling inside on an otherwise cold day at the thought of spending an evening with Mason.

Chapter Ten

Mason was getting in his dark blue Chevy Silverado after his coffee date-not-date with Lacey when someone piercingly called his name. He turned to see Millicent Jenkins hastily walking over to him. She walked up, folded her arms, and glared at him. "I see now why you canceled our date last night. Lacey's in town. I saw you two cozied up talking outside of Java House just now. You could've just told me the truth. That you're too busy chasing your ex to have spent time with me." Mason opened the truck door and took his coat off to lay it inside. "Millie, I'm not chasing my ex. You're over-reacting as usual. I canceled because I couldn't get out of something with work and I told you a few days ago....and it wasn't a date.

I told you Thanksgiving weekend that I didn't want a relationship and you said neither did you. We went out a few times. That's all. I said I'd take you to your company's dinner last night as friends, and you said you were fine with that. So, where are the jealous girlfriend theatrics coming from? " Mason was not one for drama.

"I'm sorry. I'm just upset that you backed out. Then, I saw you two together. It's none of my business." Millie was a drama queen who made everything her business, but relatively harmless. She would temporarily fall head over heels for every guy she went out with for about a month and then she would move on to the next one. She had always had a crush on Mason, but he had never returned the attraction. He recently went out with her a few times just to hang out, but she didn't move on after a few dates like he expected her to.

He had regretted his decision after the first date, but continued to see her again two or three more times. She had given him such a pitiful plea as she was skilled at playing the guilt card, and he had agreed to go with her to her company's holiday dinner. He had to go to Tennessee to work on a commercial location that they serviced, and had gotten stuck having to stay overnight. That had put him behind schedule when he returned to Fair Bend and he knew he would have to work late Friday. He did in all fairness, let her know while in Tennessee that he wouldn't be able to go. It wasn't his fault that she didn't have her usual reserve man in place.

"Millie, I am sorry that I couldn't go last night. I am. I didn't want to back out on you because that's not who I am. I'm sorry if I led you on to think there was something more happening between us. It's not. We are not going to happen. I feel like I have to say that so that you don't misunderstand. It has nothing to do with Lacey being in town. She is here for work and will be gone after Christmas. Her being here has no affect on any of this. You and I are just friends. If you act like a jealous girlfriend again, we won't even be that anymore." Mason hopped in his truck. "So, we're good here?" An embarrassed Millicent shook her head. "Yeah, we're good."

Five minutes later, she was flirting with the owner of the convertible red mustang parked next to her. He was definitely her type. Not Mason. The vixen of Fair Bend. She would not be satisfied with someone as unassuming as Mason. She thrived on the chase and wanted to be chased. It was a ripple effect of her insecurities that would keep her from ever finding happiness and contentment if she didn't learn to get past them.

Chapter Eleven

The next afternoon, Lacey was helping her mom wrap gifts for Kara and the boys. They would be flying in on the 22nd. Lacey was jubilant about spending the holidays with her entire family, although Kara's husband, Ted, wouldn't be flying in until Christmas Eve due to his work schedule.

"Do you want to help me with dinner after this? Your father is going to grill steaks and I thought we could prep a salad and bake some potatoes" Veronica suggested as she tied bows around the perfectly wrapped gifts she had neatly placed to her side. Lacey was envious of how talented her mother was as wrapping gifts. She was a pro. Lacey was terrible at it. She would usually just put gifts in decorated gift bags and be done with it. She didn't have the patience nor the time to put into wrapping. If her gifts would look as wonderful as Veronica's, maybe she would make more effort to gift wrap. "Can't. I—have plans. I won't be home for dinner tonight. I need to start getting ready soon. I thought I told you already." Lacey was getting up and starting to walk away. She was hoping to avoid the curious questioning that would surely ensue by her mother. "No, you didn't tell me. What are your plans that are obviously secretive since you haven't mentioned them and causing you to scamper off in such a rush?" the inquisitive Veronica was hot on her daughter's trail as Lacey tried to head upstairs. Veronica stood at the bottom of the staircase. Lacey turned at the top of the stairs and teased "I didn't tell you. I have a date with Prince Harry. He's flying in from London as we speak." With that, she turned on her heel in her toe socks and darted around the corner towards her bedroom.

An hour later, Lacey appeared downstairs in a pair of faux leather leggings with over-the-knee boots and a long royal blue top. "Wow, Miss Sex Goddess. Prince Harry will be quite impressed. He may have to whisk you off on a private jet back to England after your date. Don't forget your parents when you're dripping in the royal jewels." Lacey gave her mom a confused glare and stopped herself from responding as she knew her mother couldn't have realized the possible context she could've intercepted that comment. "Don't make a big deal out of this. It's just two friends going to see a Christmas play. I'm going with Mason to Charlotte to see *A Christmas* Carol. The tickets were free. He didn't buy them for me and ask me on a date or anything." Lacey was making sure to downplay their plans. "You're going with Mason to Charlotte? Didn't you have coffee with him yesterday?" Veronica was starting the inquisition. "How did you know that? I didn't even mention it because of this look you're giving me right now. It's not a big deal, mom" Lacey said with exasperation. "I'm not saying anything. You are. Thou doth protest too much, maybe? I just asked where my gorgeous single daughter was headed off to. You're the one who made plans to hang out with your first love....as friends, of course" Veronica beamed. Mason rang the doorbell. "Not a date, mom." Lacey was holding her arm behind her waving her mother away as Veronica continued to follow her.

"Hi, Mrs. Myers." "Hi, Mason" Veronica smirked. "You look--{Mason stopped himself from finishing the sentence. He didn't want to seem like he was making more of this than a night out with an old friend} " We'd better get going. I'll have your daughter back by a decent hour" Mason said holding his hand over his heart and slightly bowing. He was still so smugly charming. Lacey walked past him trying not to be obvious in noticing how handsome he was. Mason rarely dressed in anything other than an Eddie Bauer casual look. Tonight, he was wearing a burgundy sweater that zipped a few inches at the top and had it unzipped over a tank. He had a wool gray scarf hanging loosely around his shoulders. Dark jeans and leather shoes. He had a little mousse in his hair, and a hint of cologne that made Lacey tingle all over as she walked past him in the doorway. After ten years, how did he still affect her this way? She knew the feeling was mutual by the way he checked her out from head to toe. He had tried to hide his infatuation, but she knew it was there. For a moment, she felt like she was in high school all over again.

As they made their way back to Fair Bend, it began to snow. "I think it's supposed to be a light dusting tonight. Do you remember when we got caught in that storm in college when we went on that ski trip?" Mason laughed. "What a mess. We missed classes for two days because we were snowed in at that cabin. I can still see my car spinning getting zero traction and you were standing there in like five layers of clothing with our bags complaining about missing mid-terms." "Oh, God, how could I forget?" Lacey chimed in. "You had been skiing before, but I hadn't. I fell more times than I cared to count and was all banged up from not being able to stay upright. There wasn't a satellite or anything for the TV, and no one told us we needed to bring DVDs, so we had nothing to watch."

"Well, we found ways of occupying our time, I think" Mason interrupted. "Yes, we did, but with two other couples staying there, let's just say we were all ready to go by the end of the weekend and awakened to a foot of snow when it wasn't even predicted to start snowing until late that day well after we had left. At least we had plenty of junk food and those dreaded bubba burgers." "Don't knock the bubba burgers. Zeke and I share a couple about once a week." They both laughed.

"I was wondering. You'll probably think it's silly, but you know how we used to go skating at the mini ice rink down by the park when we were kids and even when we were home on winter break. I loved how they decorated the park entrance at Christmas. I was thinking about it and I want to go skating. I haven't been to an ice rink in Boston in a few years now and this year, I want to experience Christmas again. You know. Soak it all in. Would you want to go with me tomorrow? I don't have to work until later tomorrow afternoon. Never mind. I'm sure you're entirely too busy with work," Lacey said feeling as if she had asked too much of him. "Sure, Lace. I can go in tomorrow afternoon. I don't have anything that can't wait a few hours, unless I get something majorly in crisis to come in. I can't believe I'm going to go skating again. I haven't been in years, but why not? See you there about eleven?" "That sounds good," Lacey agreed.

It was starting to snow pretty heavily. Mason took Lacey's hand and wrapped it over his shoulder. "I should go inside." Lacey finally spoke. "Yeah, you should. I'm sure Veronica will be waiting for a play by play of the show of course. "Yes, the play. She'll want to know all about the play—that she's seen probably dozens of times." Lacey kidded. As Mason walked Lacey to the door of her parents' home,

Veronica and Rick peered through the curtain in the living room. Lacey noticed them and alerted Mason. "We have an audience." Mason waved to the window and smiled. "So, listen. This was fun. No worries. I'm not falling for you again after one evening." "Oh really, well, thanks." Lacey teased. Mason slowly turned and walked to his truck. Lacey watched from inside the doorway as he drove away, as Veronica leaned against her daughter's shoulder and hugged her. "So, did sparks still fly?" Lacey kissed her mom on the forehead and walked upstairs. "Good night mom. Good night dad. I love you."

Chapter Twelve

Lacey arrived at Fair Bend Park to the ice rink parking area. She could see the white snowflake lighting wrapped around the entrance line of trees that would serve as a light show of wonder at night. There were already people skating on the commercially made rink. They didn't decorate trees anymore for the safety of the deer and other animals, but did have one tree enclosed within the rink that had lights and a huge red bow streaming down from it. The lights were attached to the powered equipment and would illuminate in the evenings. Artificial snowflakes attached to the gates of the rink. It was still a beautiful setting, even if it was much more simplistic than the rinks in Boston.

Mason pulled up in his truck and walked over to join Lacey by the rink's entrance gate. "I hate to say it's been probably five years since I've been here. Ten minutes away and I ride past it all the time. It's funny how that is. It's like people who live at the beach, but never go and yet, thousands spend tons of money to visit every year to a beach spot those people could ride to in under five minutes any time they wished. It's the same with the park. I am glad it's utilized by some, but I just don't even think of coming here to hang out anymore. Looking at how much time and effort the city and county puts in to maintaining it, decorating for Christmas, and having events, I'm embarrassed that I haven't been more involved in community activities," Mason said feeling nostalgia of his youth that had faded away. They rented skates and bundled their scarves around their necks. Lacey pulled her fair isle cable knit pom hat over her ears, and put on her gloves. She zipped her North Face jacket up as far as it would go. Mason was wearing a beanie hat, but pulling it over his ears was going too far for him. He did put on gloves and zipped his Carhaart coat. "Let's see who breaks their leg first," he teased as he raced past Lacey who was struggling to stay up on the ice. She knew he was once practically an Olympic level ice skater thanks to his high school hockey days, and was saddened to hear he hadn't been to the rink in so long. It obviously hadn't tarnished his skills. After starting out slowly around the edges of the rink, Lacey gained momentum and got in her groove. She was also a talented skater. She wouldn't give Michelle Kwan a run for her money or anything, but she could do some fancy spins back in the day. It took her a few loops around for the ice to work into her skates and feel the skates bond with her feet, but once she got comfortable, she was on fire.

They skated by each other making silly faces and showing off to the college kids who weren't much more than beginners; feeling carefree as the arctic air chilled their faces. It was the most relaxed Lacey had felt in ages. Mason seemed to relish in how well he could still kick up the ice.

They met on the side against the rail for a rest. "We've still got it. You especially, Mason," Lacey applauded. "You always were a little scared to let go and throw caution to the wind. I am sure that hasn't changed, has it?" Mason probed. "Hey, it was my idea to come out here. I know how to have fun. I'm no stick in the mud," Lacey defended. "I'm not saying that. I just meant you have always been afraid of leading with your spirit and your heart. You are cautious in every detail of your life. That's all I mean. It's not a criticism, necessarily. Being cautious is often the right course, but sometimes you have to fly into the wind like you do on skates and see what happens."

"I did fly.... to Boston," Lacey rebuked. "I didn't know what would happen by taking that internship." Mason shrugged. "I meant in your personal life. You knew that internship would open doors. It wasn't much of a risk. I take it back. I haven't seen or talked to you in years. Who am I to assume to know the person you've become. I'm sure you skate in Boston and have been on blind dates, went out with friends and turned your phone off. Maybe even skydived." They both snickered. "Well, not quite all of that, but I'm working on loosening up."

"Hey, suggesting to come here was a great idea, Lace. It has been nice to spend time with you like this feeling like kids again. We both need a little spontaneity in our lives. This is what we both needed. A little down time to--"Are you OK?" Lacey tripped over her skate as she let go of the rail and Mason caught her in his arms. "I didn't mean literal down time, Lacey." They burst into laughter and she laid her head into his chest. After catching her breath, she looked up at Mason. "Thanks for the catch." "You know I'll always catch you when you fall," Mason professed. Lacey gave a flushed smile. "Let's go another round and show these kids how it's done." She skated away, as he watched her.

Almost an hour had passed and Lacey stopped to check her phone. "Oh, no. I have to get going. I need to get to Charlotte to the store." They skated up to a rest bench. "This was fun. Thanks for coming and doing this with me, today, Mason." "It was fun for me, too. "You know, you should come by and see my place. Meet Zeke. He'd like you. I mean, he likes most everyone, but I think he'd really like you." Lacey wasn't sure going to Mason's house was a good idea. It was apparent that he wanted to spend more time with her. She didn't want to mislead him. Boston was her home now. She'd be going back there very soon.

"Mason, I don't know if-I don't want any

misunderstanding of us spending time together." Mason quickly assured her that he had no agenda. "Lace, it's no big deal. Come by. Don't come by. I just wanted you to see that I've done OK for myself. I don't have the fancy apartment in Boston like you do, but I do alright. I am really proud of the work I've done renovating my grandparents' home, and I've become pretty darn good with creating furniture and working with my hands. I just wanted to show you, you know, that I'm good," he confided. "In that case, of course I'll come. I'd love to see what your hands can do. I mean, with the house," she blushed and looked away. Mason blushed as well, laughed, and took his gloves off. "I'll turn in the skates. I know you need to get going," he offered. "Thank you. I appreciate that," Lacey said in an effort to sound almost professional after her inadvertent homage to his prowess.

Chapter Thirteen

Lacey was pleased with how everything was shaping up at Romelle's. She had just completed a conference call with Mr. Tollerson and the manager of the Charlotte store, when she received a call from someone with Alberson's. She had been waiting to hear back from him regarding their meeting in Chicago earlier in the month, and was getting concerned that it had taken this long to hear anything further. "Ms. Myers, this is Paul Alberson's assistant. Mr. Alberson has gone over your proposal with our VP, Stefan Marquardt and he is ready to schedule a meeting with you to finalize the details of the spring line acquisition. "I am overseeing some inventory and design reports at our Charlotte store, but can fly up for the day later this week" Lacey offered. "He will come to you. He wants to visit a Romelle's store and spend a couple of hours learning the ins and outs of how the layout is selected for the home goods and housewares departments."

Lacey hung up a bit nervous about the VP of Alberson's coming to Charlotte. Why did he have to pick a store that had recently opened. She would've much rather they met on her own turf at the flagship store in Boston or at least at the store in Chicago. She didn't want to psyche herself out over it. At least the groundwork had been completed and the negotiations were complete for the most part. He would be coming to North Carolina on the 20th. Five days. She could do this. The store was doing well, and there was steady traffic flow and registers rolling. She had planned to be there two more days this week and could use some of that time to prepare a stronger layout focusing on those departments in specific.

She stayed over in Charlotte that night to spend some time going over the details of the Alberson project and decided to take a dinner break at a restaurant that had been raved about by the manager of Romelle's. It was a block down the street and she liked the proximity to the new store. After shopping, people want to go eat. After a lunch date, ladies want to shop. There was a deli across the street from Romelle's and a Starbucks next door. This was a good location for the store. There was a mix of independent and chain businesses that complemented each other.

As she walked past Starbucks, she almost ran smack into Alexia Dodson-Renoir. She just couldn't see her without thinking of all three names. "Lacey. Fancy running into you in the Queen City. You must be working at that chain store next door. Why did she have to say it so insultingly—*chain* store. Like it was a thrift shop that she would drop off her hand-me-downs to. Not that there was anything wrong with thrift shops. Lacey knew of some rather expensive "thrift" shops that weren't for the thrifty or those of lower incomes at all. In Boston, she had seen used designer shoes for $300 in the Thrifty Fashionista. Granted, they were over a $1000 new, but still. "Yes, Alexia. I am overseeing our newest store and am stoked about the reception to it from the great Queen City. Lots of happy holiday shoppers today. You should check it out." Lacey tapped Alexia on the hand as she encouraged her to shop with the 'common folk'.

"Yes, I will have to get around to stopping in at some point. So, where are you headed. Back to Fair Bend for the night?" Again, why did everything this woman said seem condescending. "I'm actually staying in Charlotte tonight. I have a lot of work to do in preparation for a major account I'm finalizing. Headed to grab a bite to eat. Probably should get on my way as I'm famished."

Lacey began to walk past when Alexia spun and met her shoulder to shoulder. "I'll join. My husband, you know he's a doctor, *(Yes, everyone is aware that you are married to a doctor. You just reminded me a week or so ago when I had the misfortune of running into you for the first of now two annoying encounters)* is still in California and Brinkley-Baxter is having a piano lesson and then a karate lesson at the youth center about two minutes from here. Lacey was surprised Alexia allowed her child to interact with other children. Then again, she was also surprised she had purchased him that chicken salad sandwich allowing him to eat gluten after her stance at the diner about how she wouldn't dare consume bread. Lacey knew she would be wasting her breath to try and wiggle out of this impromptu dinner with the snob of her high school.

As the two women ate their salads, Alexia received a series of text messages that made her visibly unnerved. "Is everything OK? You look a bit—concerned." Lacey wasn't sure how best to say *You look like you've seen a ghost.* "I'm fine. It's just that my husband won't be making it home for Christmas after all. He has been working at a hospital in Palm Springs for a few months after leaving his position here. He wasn't happy with the changes the hospital was making and decided to try out an offer for a temporary position. If he likes it, we will be relocating to Palm Springs. I would love a warmer climate. I'm thin and pretty, so I can fit in anywhere, naturally, and of course, we would enjoy the palm trees and the spas. He's an avid golfer and Palm Springs has fabulous courses.

I do wonder how Brinkley-Baxter would adjust as for some reason, he really likes winter and snow. Anyway, Bates, that's my husband, was supposed to come home this weekend and we were going to make a decision over the holidays." Lacey could see Alexia's eyes welling up. She guessed her mother was right. You shouldn't assume to know what someone else may be going through. Everyone has problems. "Oh well. We will just have to fly out and see him instead." Alexia tried sounding hopeful and upbeat about an obviously emotionally painful situation. "I will call him back after dinner. Of course he wants to spend Christmas with his family. He probably will call tonight and suggest we fly out this weekend and spend the week." Alexia continued to ramble on in an effort to convince herself more than Lacey that this were true. "Listen to me babbling on. I'm sure you have far more interesting topics as a career woman taking on the world one chain store at a time." *And she's back. Divert the conversation by subtle insults towards someone else. Way to deflect.*

Lacey could have retaliated and taken some digs at Alexia by continuing that conversation about why her husband probably wasn't coming back home any time soon, but she was feeling sorry for Alexia. She could see through the facade. She decided to be the bigger person and continue on. "Well, I'm a buyer and am hoping to become VP of our company soon. I'm also hoping to start a small line of my own in our home goods division of pillow covers, duvets, sofa covers, and area rugs. I like to decorate simple yet tasteful accent pieces. I want to create a line of furniture covers for pet owners and families who need or simply want to save money by dressing up their current furnishings when they can't afford or choose not to replace them. I have a portfolio of designs and samples already created for my pitch that I'm hoping to get the green light on in the new year." Lacey enjoyed discussing her creative side of design. She was a talented interior designer, but also wanted to include her own pieces in homes and businesses design layouts, as well.

"You know, that reminds me of a conversation I had last week with Millicent Jenkins. You remember Millie, right?" {How could Lacey forget such a gossiping, meddling, off-her-rocker-a-bit loose cannon like Millicent.} "Anyhoo, she and I created a committee to plan our reunion a few years ago, which we had to cancel due to lack of commitments from other fellow graduates in our class...like you, of course" Alexia pointed out with intention.

Lacey couldn't be bothered to fly home for a dinner buffet and comparison session that would highlight focus on classmates like Alexia who boasted entirely too often. Why would she want to attend a display of labeling and gossip. She could simply read social media and get the scoop for herself. That alone, was sometimes enough to make her feel the urge to throw up a bit. "Millie called to plan our meeting for the fifteen year reunion that we're trying to plan since the ten year didn't happen and mentioned that she saw you and Mason at Java House and that you two looked rather cozy. She continued to say how she ran into him afterward and casually asked him about it and that he blew it off saying you were just catching up." Lacey had to interject a comment. "I wouldn't use the word *casually; more like grilled* as Mason mentioned they had been out a few times and that she had come up to him at The Bend. No big deal. It doesn't bother me. I know how interested she has always been in Mason. We're just spending time catching up a bit while I'm here."

"She and I were discussing the reunion and since your name had come up, I remembered you wanting to be an interior designer and open your own firm like Grace Adler on Will & Grace. She was your TV inspiration, right? I just knew you would be like her. You even looked like her with your curly hair that I will tell you I was secretly jealous of."

Alexia had been on the yearbook staff and had interviewed students about their career dreams. She probably knew the entire roster of students' life plans. She knew then she planned to be a trophy wife. She was a cheerleader, homecoming queen, head of the student council among other things. There wasn't anything wrong with that, as to each her own, but she tried so hard to outshine everyone in high school that she was likely quite miserable underneath it all. Kind of like now.

"Lacey, you should still do that. Design your own pieces and open your own interior design firm. I have several friends in both the corporate market and my ladies who redecorate their homes regularly. Being a doctor's wife gives me many connections with some extremely wealthy people who would line up for an exclusive designer. I can help market you to build that reputation and get you some accounts." Alexia was offering to help someone else. Sure, she would say how she discovered Lacey and who knows what else, but she actually seemed genuine in her offer. Lacey was starting to see there was more to Alexia than she had always thought.

"Thanks, Alexia. I have considered that. In college, I had wanted to do it my way and open my own firm by 30, but we had a recession going on and home construction was considerably down. People weren't spending money on interior designers and I chose a path that I thought would keep me employed. I don't regret my choice. I would love to think I could go out on my own, as of course that's still my dream, but I've worked a long time to get to the position that I'm about to be offered, at least that I hope I'm offered, and walking away to go it alone would be a huge risk.

I took a risk moving to Boston, but it was one that would ensure me steady opportunities and it was less risky than my alternative. I do appreciate the vote of confidence though." Lacey was rather surprised that Alexia was taking an interest in her work after just insulting her 'retail job'.

"I would love to see some of your portfolio samples. You should stop by this week after work and take a look at my main living room. I have three living spaces that are for social use and I am sure the entertaining room for guests could use sprucing up in its' décor." Alexia was determined not to drop this subject.

Lacey knew she was likely more motivated by loneliness and wanting to have company, but she found herself agreeing to stop by. She also wanted to get a peek inside the mansion of a house Alexia lived in. She was sure there were many rooms she could design new looks for. Couldn't hurt to check it out. She may get some inspiration and add to her portfolio, which could only help her convince Mr. Tollerson to give her a line of her own after becoming VP.

Chapter Fourteen

Lacey had been prepping for her meeting with Mr. Marquardt Tuesday and had agreed to visit Alexia late that afternoon. She did relish the idea of having her own design firm. Alexia was totally right when she had talked about Lacey's plan to be the next Grace Adler. She smiled thinking about her teenage dreams. She was greeted by a housekeeper at Alexia's huge home, and while waiting for Alexia, she wandered around the foyer and peeked cautiously into the living space she could see was for guests.

It was a sophisticated style that definitely gave the "we've got tons of money" message, but was not inviting at all. The blue and grey tones were a little off-putting, much like Alexia, but could easily transition with a few yellow or coral pieces mixed in to warm it up a bit. Again, much like Alexia, the room had some good points and bad, but if you tweaked it a bit you get a different feel. It was sort of how Lacey was starting to see past the pretentiousness of Alexia and see the softer side, although with Alexia there would always be some level of pretension.

She noticed elegant framed art pieces in every
room, as she peered further into the library and
dining room, after Alexia called down to "Take
a look around downstairs. I'll be down in a
sec." Granted, these rooms were formal rooms,
but she had seen no sign of anyone residing in
the home thus far. Where was the Christmas
tree? She had only seen a wreath on the door
and garland along the wooden rails of a marble
staircase. The house was like a museum. It was
hard to imagine a child lived there. Antiques
and glass trinkets that were certainly worth a
fortune were the only decorative items other
than furniture and paintings.

"Hi, Lacey. I was completing a live video of my
evening 10 minute fitness workout and so
you're catching me in my leisure look. Do
pardon my appearance. I figured you wouldn't
mind, as you seem to love the athleisure style
from what I can tell. Brinkley is at his tutoring
session down the street with a teacher who just
moved in after marrying a high powered
attorney. She quit teaching to focus on starting
a family, as of course I had to get the full scoop
when she moved in. She's only twenty-five. He
has a daughter two years younger than that.
She's doing a good job with Brinkley-Baxter's
math tutoring and she bought my fitness dvd
and attends my online sessions, so I think she's
a peach. Follow me into the kitchen while I fix
a juice detox. You should try one." Alexia
barely drew breath as she raced by on full
adrenaline. Lacey followed Alexia into the

kitchen as she flipped her the finger behind her back, catching the eye of the housekeeper in the hallway dusting. The housekeeper held back a giggle, as Lacey stuck her tongue out making a funny face. Alexia just couldn't control herself sometimes. Sure, she had seen Lacey in her sweats the first weekend she was home, but what about yesterday when she was dressed in a black dress with a red belt and Louboutin heels-heels she had rewarded herself with back in November after closing several deals. The dress and belt had come from Romelle's. She did prefer the leisure look on weekends, but she had to promote fashion most of the time as although she was a buyer in home goods and housewares, she represented every department of the store. Besides, her athleisure look was very on trend.

Lacey forced down the green juice filled with chunks of veggies. She did go through a juicing phase with Darcy, but that was about two years ago and didn't last long. She was in good shape, and generally ate well, and consumed tons of water, but she didn't get consumed with every health trend she heard of. Darcy was all about the gym. She went every day after work when she could. She was Lacey's motivator, as without Darcy, Lacey doubted she would've kept a membership. She rarely was home to use it. Long days that turned into nights at the office and travel for work left little time and she reserved personal time for red wine, reading, and watching a little TV. She tried to get in a run a few times per week during the warmer months, but rarely made it to the gym. She preferred being outside to work out. Her favorite activity had become SUP yoga (on paddle boards) on the Charles River.

"So, you've toured around the south of the house. How about we head north to the west side. *North? South? West side? Of course, she labels her house using cardinal directions. If she didn't, she'd probably lose Brinkley-Baxter.* "Lead the way" Lacey motioned. She followed Alexia up the winding stairs. *What? No elevator?* she thought sneering to herself as she walked up the stairs to the sitting area by the large bay window at the top. Lacey really did love that. "This is perfect, Alexia. I love the sitting area with the chaise lounger and plush pillow by the window overlooking your garden area. I don't want to sound rude, *although Alexia never minded doing so,* but I wouldn't take you for a gardener gal."

"I know, who would've thought, right? I started it last year with Brinks. He was having some issues focusing in school and other tasks and I was looking for a way to grow my fitness from home business, and I do love cooking with fresh veggies and juicing, so I decided to start a garden as it seemed like a good way to get him occupied doing something outdoors that could be healthy, as well. My husband got our landscaper to meet with a gardener to get it started. The gardener helped us last year, but this year, Brinks and I worked in it totally on our own. He loves working in the garden, so I've learned to love it too. Initially, I was going to let Brinks work with the gardener and not really get my hands dirty literally, but one day I was feeling-well, you know, we all have a day here and there, and I just got into it after that. Shall we check out the family room?" Alexia once again shifted the topic of conversation before it became too personal.

Lacey hated to admit she was impressed by the many rooms and the colossal pool out back, but from a designer's view, it would be a dream project and open doors for many referrals to come. Lacey considered for a moment the possibility of the "what if" scenario. As she made notes and took a few photographs, she was already envisioning small details that would make major impacts in the look and feel of the house. She knew Alexia wanted it to be luxurious, but she had hinted to making it a tad more cozy.

Lacey was pulled out of her trance of design ideas by Alexia stopping at a standstill at a closed door. "I want a more welcoming décor in the event that we put the house on the market as we need to make it more attractive to buyers. My husband and I adore our current style throughout, but I'm not sure Brinkley-Baxter is as thrilled with it. If we were to sell, I think it needs to be a little more relaxing I guess. It feels a bit--" Lacey felt the word roll off her tongue without any ability to stop. "Stuffy?" Alexia gave her a stern look, but then softened. "Yes, well, I guess that is the word, isn't it?" "I'm sorry, Alexia. I shouldn't have said that. I didn't mean—it's just a bit sophisticated for children and pets if you know, you sell and those type of families consider buying." Lacey was back-peddling anxiously. "You're right. It's stuffy. We don't even have a tree downstairs. There's one in Brinkley's room because he wanted one. I'm not *permitted* to put one up downstairs until the 22nd. What kind of random date is that? What's so darn significant about the 22nd?

I asked him why and Bates said it's a few days before Christmas and the date he grew up putting up the tree with his family. His parents don't even put up a tree anymore. Heck, we haven't been to see them in three years at all and they just send money for Brinkley. No gift. Money! Like that's what a child his age wants. He doesn't need money. We have plenty of money! He wants a train set or something that he can unwrap and play with.

Anyway, you're absolutely right about the house. It's not my style. It's his style. This room with the door closed is his private office. Supposedly, there are confidential records of some type in there and we are not to go in there. What doctor who practices in a hospital keeps confidential records in his house? It's poppycock. He just wants a room that no one goes in but himself to lock us out of when he wants to be alone. Dr. Don Juan; who's probably in Palm Springs decorating a house with a younger version of me as we speak." She stood facing the closed door and slammed her hands against it letting out a scream. Alexia suddenly burst into tears. She shared her anger and sadness with Lacey for the next half an hour trying to hold back more tears. For someone who was always so perfectly posh and in control, Lacey was in shock witnessing this breakdown of sorts as she wondered why she had to be present for it.

Lacey knew that Alexia likely had no real friends and in her circle of acquaintances, she wouldn't dare confide in any one for fear of being shunned. It was like being invited to attend a live showing of a downfall of a member of one of the reality housewives television shows. This must be why they act insane on those shows. Cheating husbands, scandals, backstabbing. Maybe it wasn't fake, after all, as Lacey had previously thought.

After the drama-filled home tour had ended with a glass of wine and a somewhat awkward hug and cheek kiss that Lacey wasn't sure she did correctly, she was headed back to Fair Bend. At least she felt she had cheered Alexia up by the time she left. She hoped she had been helpful. Alexia did say she was going to have her personal assistant come over and decorate the Christmas tree and take Brinkley shopping after school for some fun ornaments for his tree. True she wouldn't decorate it personally, but at least she was going to defy Dr. Don Juan, although he wasn't going to be here for Christmas anyway. She did point out that she was going to send him a picture of the tree just so he would know she put it up earlier than the 22nd. Lacey didn't envy that lifestyle whatsoever. She wanted simplicity. She wanted......

She decided to call Mason as it had been two days and he was awaiting a reply to his invitation to dinner...at his house. No theatre filled with patrons, no busy cafe' or coffee house, just the two of them for dinner. Alone. Well, them and Zeke, of course. He would have to be the buffer if...when...things turned romantic.

Chapter Fifteen

December 18th.....

Lacey was feeling nervous about her dinner date with Mason. This felt like it was going to be a date. She had insisted to her parents that it was just dinner and they were friends, but she wasn't sure she believed that herself. She loved Boston. Mason was in Fair Bend. She let him go years ago. It would be callous to hurt him again, and she knew he still had feelings for him. He was the one initiating spending time together. It was obvious there was more than friendship going on between them despite him assuring her that he wasn't naive about her short stay in Fair Bend. She had been clear with him about not wanting to mislead him. They had agreed they were just friends now.

As she looked into the bathroom mirror as she finished applying her makeup, she stopped and stared at her reflection. She didn't feel like she was going to see a friend. She had male friends in Boston. This didn't feel like hanging out and watching sports at a tavern drinking Sam Adams. This felt like getting ready for a date. She wasn't sure if the pit she was starting to feel in her stomach was from hunger pangs as she hadn't eaten since she had a bagel that morning or from the attraction she still felt after all these years toward Mason.

It could be that the nervousness she felt was from the adrenaline of too much caffeine after two cups of coffee that morning with the pumpkin spice bagel her mom had made-she really should open a bakery, but insists she's too busy helping out with the bookkeeping at the hardware store. Later, there was the salted caramel mocha she had gotten for free as a holiday drink giveaway that afternoon when she left the hardware store after she had surprised her dad with lunch for him.

She had been in a thousand hurries with calls and emails and had spent most of the morning working from Java House on her laptop and on the phone in her rental Lexus. The mocha had been her sugar and caffeine pick-me-up. No, this feeling was more akin to the love-stricken twinges known as *butterflies*. She would ignore them. They would go away. She would only be in town through Christmas. She would be back in Boston in just over a week. She had hoped to stay through most of the weekend following Christmas and drive up Sunday the 29th.

Knowing Mr. Tollerson, he may expect her to drive back on the 26th to attend a Friday meeting, but she was hoping to delay her return through the weekend as it should benefit her that she drove down on a company paid rental or he would surely expect her to fly back and be in his office first thing Friday morning. She was thinking about work to distract her weird emotions.

She didn't really have butterflies with Cooper. It made sense to date. They made financial and career sense together. He was the only somewhat serious relationship she had been in since moving to Boston. Lacey pondered for a moment how pathetic that may seem, but being in a relationship had not been her focus. That's why she ended her relationship with Mason in the first place. It wasn't because she didn't love him. She made the choice to focus on her career. She wouldn't be ashamed of that. Her success didn't come without sacrifices.

As she changed clothes again before settling on a casual look, skinny jeans, Ugg short boots, and a black sweater that laced up the back-she wanted to be a little sexy without appearing as though she was trying too hard or thought of this as a date. She had changed out of two outfits already thinking one was too dressy for dinner at someone's home, and the other for being too "come hither" of a look. The stiletto heels and cold shoulder boob-hugging top were not going to work. "Where did this top come from anyway?" She thought as she tossed it across the bed. "Darcy, of course." Darcy had relentlessly carried on about Lacey showing up any frenemies from the past or making old flames jealous and had packed a few items that Lacey had bought but never worn into her bag.

Lacey didn't really have any arch enemies from the past. It was just Darcy's way of trying to get her some spicy outfits for the trip home in case she met a man in Charlotte and had some fun or saw Mason. Darcy had always held out hope for Lacey that one day Mason would show up in Boston and profess his undying love. The hopeless Hallmark movie romantic. She was completely unabashed about her tactics in playing Cupid.

Chapter Sixteen

"Wow! This is so serene." Lacey was admiring the wrap-around porch of Mason's mountain styled cabin two story home and landscaping surrounding it. "There's a huge pond in the back that looks like a lake from the house. It's harder to see in the summer when the trees are full with leaves, but it's a nice view this time of year now that *Old Man Winter* has arrived. I must say, fall is probably my favorite season for sitting on the deck out back. I have a large print framed in my workshop of the pond that I took last fall." Mason beamed with pride.

"I inherited the property from my grandparents and moved in shortly after my divorce a few years ago. I kept much the same as far as the original exterior, although I added the porch. "I love the rocking chairs and swing. Did you make those?" Lacey knew Mason had mentioned he was doing woodworking and making furniture on the side. "Yes. I have actually sold several rocking chairs at the marketplace in Fair Bend. I had several custom orders from people in Charlotte and Boone this year after the spring fair.

Our little town has become somewhat of a tourist attraction for our spring and fall festivals and people come from a couple of hours away on weekends to check out local handmade items at the marketplace." Mason was impressing Lacey with his talent and she was feeling butterflies again. She was in trouble and hadn't even made it inside the house yet. "You are really talented, Mason." She touched his shoulder and smiled.

"I do love the garland wrapped all around the porch. You're one of the rare men who decorate for Christmas. Most men who have bachelor pads don't concern themselves with holiday decorating," she teased. "I wish I could take the credit and appear as a modern man of every woman's dream, but truthfully my mother deserves the kudos. I did, in fact, wrap the garland, and the tree you will see inside, I did buy and set up. That's about the extent of my participation in the wonderland you see before you." He laughed and pointed toward the large wreath of burlap and greenery with a red bow at the bottom. Mom made the wreath. She sells them at the marketplace at my booth. I think your mom bought one from her last weekend. She added my house to a home tour for her church group and they are coming by tomorrow evening. I don't mind. It looks nice, I guess. I like Christmas decorations, but yes, I'm the typical guy when it comes to decorating. It's pretty to look at, but tedious to set up and take down everything."

Zeke ran around the corner to greet them. "Hey boy. Meet Lacey." The black Labrador was wagging his tail and rubbing against Mason's leg. "Hi there Zeke. I've heard good things." Lacey teased rubbing him on the head as he nudged her back and turned in a circle. "He loves his back scratched." Mason leaned over and gave him a scratch as Lacey joined in.

"Come inside and I'll show you around." He proceeded with a tour of his home showing Lacey the bar, the dining table, and a mantle over the fireplace that he had crafted. Lacey was in awe of this talent she had never been privy to seeing. "I remember you always tinkering with things and being quite the handyman as a teenager, but I don't recall you making anything out of wood. When did you get into woodworking? This is truly a calling for you." Lacey complimented Mason as she continued touring the home. "I guess it started after I moved back. I needed something more in my life other than the electrical business and to be honest, you were in some way, my muse. I mean that in a positive way. You were so passionate about life and so sure of yourself, and you set goals. Even if they seemed to shift into a different direction, you were determined to succeed. You seized opportunities and I wanted to find something I felt that ambition for. Working as an electrician is fine as being an engineer was really never my dream. I wanted a reason to go to college and knew I would learn beneficial skills from my classes, but I'm more hands-on. I think that's what led me to woodworking and building furniture. I wanted something to put energy into that made me feel accomplished, creative, and that I made with my own hands.

After you left, I felt empty, Lacey I was hurt and things with my family were in turmoil. It was rough for a while. I started out making a simple bread bin for my mom and a kitchen knife holder for dad. They were so happy and boasted about it to everyone they knew that I started getting requests.

At first, I stuck to the small stuff. Magazine racks, trash bins, and small wine racks. Then, over the past few years, I've gotten into much more. I took some classes at the community college and read some books. Honestly, most of it just comes naturally to me."

Mason walked over to the bar and pressed his hands against it from the opposite side of Lacey. He looked even more kissable than he did when he caught her hand on his chest a few nights ago after their evening in Charlotte. He was in a gray sweater and jeans. A little moused curls in the front of his hair.

Lacey eased herself onto a bar stool as she attempted to break her gaze at Mason. "I know you were a fan of red wine back in college. Is Cabernet OK?" "Cabernet works for me." Lacey chimed in hoping to appear oblivious to his charm. He poured the wine. "Dinner smells delicious. Chicken?" Lacey was starving and wanted a reason to move further apart as Mason had pulled up a stool on the other side of the bar and was facing her as they sipped the best Cabernet Sauvignon she had ever tasted. Maybe it tasted so good because the company was the best she could ask for.

"Yes, it's roasted honey glazed chicken with cubed sweet potatoes and a side of green beans with yeast rolls. I like to keep it simple. You're probably used to duck confit or lobster tails and fancy side dishes. Please don't tell me you're a vegetarian or vegan or no-carb because I didn't think to ask ahead of time. If you are, I've got veggies to make a salad. I can whip up some dirt and water to make a weird soup if none of those work." He burst into laughter.

"Ha.Ha. Very funny. The menu sounds perfect. Actually, everything looks so inviting. Have you been taking entertaining courses or something?" Lacey retorted as they began a flirtatious banter.

"Seriously, Mason. The candles on the dining table, the wine, which is just divine by the way. The smell of the food...you know how to impress a girl. Then again, you've always known how to do that." They took another sip of wine and kept their eyes on each other.

"Let's try that chicken. I'm pretty famished." Lacey placed her glass on the bar and walked over to smell the food on the stove. "Well, I can't be known as the guy who keeps a woman waiting when she's hungry, now can I?" Mason remarked walking up behind Lacey. She could feel his breath on her neck and smell his subtle cologne as he leaned around her. She turned around facing him unsure of what his intention was. "I was just going to get the plates from the cabinet," Mason said with a slight smile. She blushed with embarrassment.

"Oh, sure. I mean, I didn't realize you were so..you know, close behind me. I was just going to ask where you kept the dishes." She wasn't going to ask. She thought he was going to kiss her. Mason knew it, as well. They stood there facing each other only inches away from each other, neither moving for what seemed like minutes, although it was only a few seconds. Mason reached over Lacey's shoulder. "I'll just get the plates now." Lacey swiftly moved across the kitchen.

Mason served dinner and poured a second glass of wine for the two of them. This was the best non-date Lacey had ever been on. Candlelit dinner. Dim lighting. Wine. A delicious meal and an equally delicious man sitting across from her.

After dinner, Lacey and Mason walked out back onto the deck that extended from the wrap-around porch and down to the concrete pad where a fire pit and Adirondack chairs created a cozy outdoor entertaining area. Lacey took notice of all aspects of interior and exterior design and décor in every home she visited. The pieces they chose, the paint colors, the style of home often reflected the personality of the homeowner. Even those who had more modest means often found little detail objects that were of meaning or interest to the person. Mason was a country boy. A lover of nature and serenity. However, he liked personal attachment to his home and his simplistic style was definitely indicative of a man's space, but also showed his out-of-the-box craftsmanship and creative style.

They sat down with their Cabernet and Mason started a fire. Zeke came up for a moment and then ran off with a toy Mason threw to him. He had brought out a blanket for Lacey to wrap over her to ward off the chill of a brisk December night. It wasn't extremely cold as there had been a warm-up, but it wouldn't have likely mattered either way. Lacey was nice and toasty being next to Mason. She wasn't sure if the warm, tingly sensation she felt was from drinking the wine or from sitting there looking up at the full moon and twinkling stars, listening to the crackling fire, and talking to the man she had walked away from a decade ago.

Lacey lifted her feet up on the chair and laid the blanket across her. "I could get used to this.

It's so peaceful out here. I could almost fall asleep. I've almost forgotten how nice it is to sit out in the countryside with only the sounds of nature in your ear. The moon shines so much more brightly in the country. The darkness offset by a light show of stars to guide your way home." She stood and wrapped the blanket over her shoulders continuing to gaze at the evening sky. "I can see the constellations. I never even look at the sky in Boston anymore. I usually am looking at skyscrapers instead. It's mesmerizing, isn't it?"

Mason walked up behind her and wrapped his arms around her to warm her. He was awestruck by her beauty as he kept his eyes focused on her illumination by the firelight. "Yes, mesmerizing is the word I'd choose." Lacey leaned back into his chest acknowledging his compliment. "You're welcome to stay the night. No expectations. If for no other reason than to get your mom's curiosity on overload, you should stay." "That would definitely get mom's attention. She would be waiting by the door tomorrow morning." They both began to laugh. Mason leaned into Lacey's neck and she could feel his warm breath as she continued to look up at the clear evening sky. "Just letting you know the offer stands."

"Oh, look, Mason. A family of deer are over by the yard light," Lacey interrupted diverting the subject and stepping away. Mason smiled while playing along. He knew he still affected her.

"Yeah, I bet you don't get many deer in the woods or crickets in the summer living in a busy city like Boston." "No, more like sirens and horns. However, we do have beautiful skyscraper buildings that are quite glorious, especially this time of year. I do love to see Boston at Christmas. I love it here too, though. I guess the saying of roots and wings is true. You can love both where you came from and where you have been led."

"So, you're happy, Lace? I mean, in Boston. Is it all you hoped it would be living somewhere so far away from Fair Bend?" "I'm happy-ish. I don't know. It's so strange. I thought I was on track and things were lining up just as they should. Ducks in a row and all that. Then, I came home and it's been different this time. Alexia Dodson and I have been discussing an interior design business. She offered to help me with referrals and even gave me my first project; her home. It got me contemplating things. I haven't thought about my own firm in years. I closed the book on that idea a long time ago. Lately, I've started reconsidering. Reconsidering many things, in fact. I guess, you don't miss what you don't have. I never allow myself to spend much time here or think about what I left behind {Lacey paused and looked at Mason}..or who I left."

"I don't think about you either. At least, not often. I did. I did all the time for a while and then I stopped. I got the letter you sent me that fall telling me about your friend, Darcy, how well things were going with the internship, how much you were enjoying Boston, and the offer for you to start a full time position after the internship ended. It was obvious to me you weren't coming back." Mason said with sadness. "I didn't know you were waiting. We agreed that our lives were going in different directions and that we would resent each other if I didn't go." Lacey knew she was the one to blame for the past, but she had always wondered why Mason didn't fight harder to convince her to stay. "I wanted you to go with me, but-"

"You didn't ask me to go with you Lacey!" Mason stood and walked over to the fire and chunked it. His frustration was obvious. "I didn't know it was an option, Mason. You were going back home to help your family's business. You wouldn't have deserted them and followed me. I couldn't have asked you to do that. It would have been selfish. I was already being selfish." Lacey walked over in front of him. "I know I couldn't have gone. It's not the point. The point is that you didn't even put the possibility on the table." He paused. "It doesn't matter. We were practically still kids. We had never dated anyone else. We had spent five years together and at our age, we probably shouldn't have. You were right to go. I was right to stay. Ten years have come and gone and I've been fine until I saw you at The Bend

by the fountain. The fountain of all places."
Mason turned to face Lacey.

"I know. It was where we had our first kiss. I
remembered. I just didn't allow myself to think
about it. Every time I see you, I start having
thoughts of what was, what may have been, and
I stop myself each time before I admit...."Lacey
was finally coming to terms with the truth.

"Admit what, Lacey." Mason reached for her
hands. "Admit that I still have feelings for you.
I guess I've never stopped having feelings. I
don't know what exactly they are, but I still
feel... something...every time I've seen you or
have talked to you since I've been here." Lacey's
eyes started to well up, as Mason pulled her
close to him. He wanted to kiss her. She wanted
him to kiss her.

Their lips touched softly for a moment. Mason
pulled Lacey in close and wrapped his arms
around her, kissing her passionately this time.
After a few seconds, Lacey pulled away. "I have
to go." She turned and ran up the steps of the
deck into the house. Mason followed. "Why?
Why do you have to go? Lacey, stop for a
second" Mason said taking her hands and
gently leaning her to a chair in the living room.
"We both know you're going back to your life in
Boston. I know one kiss or even one night
together isn't going to change your plans. I'm
not that naive. You don't have to go. Just stay."
Mason pleaded.

"I can't. I shouldn't have come over. It was a bad idea. Thank you for dinner. You have a lovely home" Lacey grabbed her coat and headed for the door fighting against her heart's desire to stay. She watched Mason standing on the porch in her rear view mirror as she drove away.

So many emotions were racing through her mind. She didn't want to hurt Mason again. She didn't want to allow herself to get hurt. She didn't want to face the truth. She was still in love with Mason Peters. Ten years hadn't made a difference in her heart. He was still the one she wanted, but her life was in Boston. His life was in Fair Bend. It was the same situation as they faced years ago. Nothing had changed. They still couldn't be together.

She sat in her driveway for a few minutes hoping to clear her head. She pulled herself together and called Darcy. She needed her best friend more than ever.

Chapter Seventeen

"Darcy, I'm losing my mind." Lacey spent the next fifteen minutes filling Darcy in on the mixed up soap opera that was becoming her life. "I didn't even know you had seen Mason but once that first weekend you were there. Why didn't you tell me about the other times or about this dinner at his house you were going to tonight?" Darcy was feeling clueless as her best friend and roommate was never forthcoming with enough information until she was about to explode.

"I didn't want to talk about him because I didn't want to analyze my feelings. I knew I wanted to see him, but I kept telling myself we were just friends. I told him that, as well, and he said he was fine with it. Sure, we had a few moments, but that's normal right? He was my boyfriend for five years, after all. Then, tonight, things were just..different. He made me dinner..by candlelight, Dar. Candlelight! "He cooked for you?" Darcy asked with delight. "Yes, and he had Cabernet. He remembered I prefer red and my favorite vino of choice. Then, we were outside by the fire, yes, a fire, and then, we kissed. Intensely. I mean, how much more of a seduction scene could there have been and then I ruined it. I just...left. I left him there watching me drive away just like he did ten years ago!"

"Lacey, oh my gosh. You're still in love with him. He obviously feels the same way. If you ask me, you two seem to have this kind of magnetic chemistry. You can't seem to stay away from each other, so why are you fighting it?"

Darcy was absolutely right. Lacey had been thinking about Alexia's offer to help her get started with a design firm and wondering if she really wanted to stay in Boston after all. She had avoided giving much real thought to anything other than Romelle's since she had been home because she was afraid. Afraid of everything changing and for once, not feeling completely in control.

"I've worked hard to get to this point and if I keep my feelings for Mason at bay, I will stay on point. I moved to Boston with plans. Plans that I haven't faltered from until now. Now, I'm having these thoughts of opening my own design firm again. Something I haven't thought about since college. I have a friend, although I'll use that word a bit loosely, who offered to help me get started with a design firm here. She has very wealthy connections and could truly be an asset if I were to call in the favors from her. I don't know what to do anymore. For once, I don't know what I want."

"Sleep on it. You'll make the right decision. No reason to rush any of it. Give yourself a break. Just see how the rest of the trip goes and see where your heart leads you. If it's back to Boston, great. If it's moving back to Fair Bend, that's fine too. Just let the cards fall where they may for once, Lace." That was easier said than done for Lacey.

As Lacey slipped inside the house careful not to wake her parents, she changed into her pajamas and fixed a cup of chamomile tea. She reached in a drawer and found old photo albums. She looked through them reminiscing. There were photos of her with Mason. There was an album of pictures she had cut out of magazines and turned into a design scrapbook from high school that was labeled *Pillows and Lace Designs*. She had created the name for her own interior design firm all those years ago. She heard Darcy's voice in her head again *let the cards fall where they may*.

She fell asleep that night while holding a photo of Mason at the fountain she had taken just before their first kiss and her scrapbook next to her on the bed.

Chapter Eighteen

Lacey had kept busy the past couple of days after the romantic evening with Mason that she had brought to a screeching halt with her typical overthinking and the constant need to keep her distance from anyone who could derail her plans. She had spent the remainder of the weekend preparing for her meeting Monday with the VP of Alberson's and helping her mom get the rooms ready for her sister and kids. They had watched a couple of Hallmark movies that her dad poked fun at, but she knew he secretly enjoyed watching. She had tried not to think of Mason, although the romantic happily-ever-after movies weren't helping. Veronica had quizzed her about her evening with Mason, but Lacey had brushed her off and simply asked for Mason to be off limits in conversation for the weekend.

It was now the 21st and she had her meeting with Stefan Marquardt that afternoon. She would get this deal done with Alberson's. Then, maybe she could devote some time to Darcy's advice of taking it day by day for the rest of the time she was in Fair Bend. This was also the last day she would be working at the

Charlotte store of Romelle's.

After she prepared her final notes for the meeting, she checked her phone that she had kept tucked away in her handbag. A voicemail from mom. A text from Darcy wishing her luck with her meeting. A text from Alexia wanting to schedule a meeting to discuss her ideas for Alexia's redecorating that she had sent over in a proposal. Lacey had not given herself time to think about Mason. Still, she was hopeful she would hear from him. She wanted to call and apologize for leaving so abruptly, but how would she explain her reason for doing so? He probably didn't want to hear from her anyway she had told herself. He would be better off if she stayed away.

As she was informed of Mr. Marquardt's arrival, she put her phone away, tucked her white blouse into her black pencil skirt and, took a deep breath. "You've got this" she reassured herself as she looked in the antique framed mirror in her temporary office.

A debonair business man greeted her at the door. "Ms. Myers. Nice to finally meet you. I've heard good things from my grandfather about your impeccable taste in interior design." Stefan Marquardt was very charming. One of those, dreamy handsome men that probably closed every deal he was involved in. Both professionally and personally. "Nice to meet you, as well, Mr. Marquardt." He interrupted her. "Please, call me Stefan." "Glad you were able to fit in a meeting with me, and I am confident you will find our offer to be mutually beneficial and unique to other competitors." "Shall we do a walk-through of our store and I'll share some numbers with you along the way." "Lead the way," Stefan replied as he motioned towards the escalator.

The meeting came to an end over an hour later and Lacey felt satisfied in her presentation. "I do hope you're impressed with our proposal, Stefan." "Yes, Lacey, I'm quite impressed. With the proposal, the inventory placement ideas, and with you. You are a gem. Romelle's is lucky to have you." "Thank you. I am pleased to hear that. Be sure to send that memo to my boss," she joked as she was starting to relax feeling secure in the progression of the business relationship forming with the two companies.

"I hope you don't find this presumptuous, but I would enjoy company for dinner. If you aren't otherwise engaged, would you care to join me? I hate to eat alone." Lacey wasn't sure whether to join him or not. She had work dinners from time to time, but usually not with such handsome men. She didn't want to give him the impression this would be anything other than business. "It's just dinner. The deal is done, and papers are signed. I just thought we could share a meal to celebrate our mutual collaboration." "Sure. Why not? Just give me a few minutes to freshen up and I'll meet you downstairs. There is a nice bistro just across the street." Lacey went to her temporary office and shut the door and let out a sigh. She was relieved this was now complete. The papers had been signed and she had them already submitted by a messenger service back to Mr. Tollerson in Boston. The store was running like a well oiled machine so far and the staff seemed knowledgeable and well chosen. She would stop by and clear her desk tomorrow when she would pick Kara and the twins up from the airport.

She grabbed her white coat and floppy hat. She hadn't worn the hat since her arrival, but today she wanted that extra dose of good luck and once again, it served her well. *Nothing wrong with a good luck charm* she had thought when she put it on that morning.

She greeted Stefan at the side entrance to the home goods department where he was surveying the inventory once more making notes. "Shall we?" He opened the door for Lacey and they walked across to the bistro.

As they sat conversing over how they both got started with their careers, their educational backgrounds, and usual topics of business dinners, someone happened to be shopping at Romelle's who had seen them walk out together. The curious woman had followed in the distance to see them enter the bistro and walked by with her coat collar pulled up hoping to go unnoticed as she walked passed the window. It was Millicent Jenkins. The drama queen of Fair Bend had to be the one to see Lacey with a handsome stranger. Lacey didn't see her peeking in from outside.

After dinner, Stefan and Lacey shook hands. "I look forward to working with your team, Lacey." "The line will be in great hands with Romelle's." Lacey added.

She drove back to Fair Bend feeling joyful that the remainder of her time in her hometown would be spent with her family and feeling accomplished and pleased with herself. However, she wished she could call Mason. She checked her phone again before leaving Charlotte and still no word from him. Maybe it was for the best. If he didn't contact her, it would make it easier for her to leave as long as she kept her distance from him.

Chapter Nineteen

Lacey was awakened to the sound of Christmas music blaring from the kitchen downstairs, and the smell of eggs and bacon. She got up and peered around the corner to see her mom dancing around the kitchen singing and her dad having coffee at the kitchen table reading the paper. He would be heading to the hardware store soon, and Lacey rushed down in her red flannel pajamas to have coffee with him and share the morning news like she did growing up.

"I miss newspapers," she said leaning down to give her father a squeeze around his neck. "I miss you, daddy. I miss our daddy-daughter mornings at this table. I know I've been so busy and spent several nights in Charlotte while I've been here, but I do want both of you to know how much it really means to me to be here and to have spent these past couple of weeks in our house, in my old room, even though I'm still in shock you haven't turned it into a craft room or something, mom. You really should. It's your space, now. Not mine." Veronica danced over to Lacey and gave her a kiss on the cheek and did the same to Rick, catching him by surprise. "It's always going to be your space, dear, even if I do change it. Don't worry. I use it for other things. Your bed is usually where I dump the laundry until I get around to putting everything away. I also keep gifts in there, and I go lounge and read. It makes me feel close to my baby. Kara and Ted visit for a week every Christmas and every other year for Thanksgiving so I keep her room fixed for them and the boys have stayed in your room when you haven't been here. You know, Ted's mother is Jewish, so they don't do as much for Christmas as we do. His dad celebrates Christmas, though, so they do a little combo of both. They usually fly out to see Kara & Ted for a weekend in early December if Kara and Ted don't fly to see them for Thanksgiving for a few days. The boys love celebrating Hanukkah and Christmas. They feel like little princes with all the gifts." Veronica poured juice and sat down at the table with them.

"We have only seen them twice, you know. The wedding and the hospital when the boys were born. I don't know much about them, but they seem like nice enough folks to me. Those are the only times you've seen them, too, right?" Rick chimed in. "Yes. Kara and I don't get to talk as often as I'd like. When we do, it's usually rushed from her end or mine. She doesn't mention Ted's parents often, so I guess that means she gets along with them or you know Kara. She would be fussing about them. She's not one to keep her opinions to herself." They all laughed heartily.

As they ate their breakfast and discussed the morning news, the morning sun shone in from the glass pane windows of the back door leading onto the deck. Lacey looked up from her plate and glanced at her parents as they talked about the hardware store and discussed errands. She wished she had someone to share her morning coffee with. Someone to laugh at her when she danced around the kitchen who would be there for her when she needed comfort, as well. She felt fortunate that her parents had stayed together all these years and that they still had a twinkle in their eyes when they would tease each other about the most trivial of things.

After clearing the table and doing the dishes, Lacey wrapped her father's coat around her and stepped in her mother's LL Bean rubber and leather boots. She stepped onto the deck with her coffee mug and gazed out at the frost on the grass and the horses with their winter coats draped around them across the field at the neighbor's ranch as they were eating hay. It was cold and windy. Not Boston blustery, but pretty strong. She thought of Mason's home and how beautiful it must look with the frosty view of the pond in the distance. She turned and went inside as she felt the chill setting in on her face.

It was time to get ready and pick up Kara and the boys from the airport as they would be arriving in a couple of hours. She had offered to pick them up so they would only need one rental car when Ted flew in. She also needed to call Alexia to go over the details of her design board and she had a call scheduled for 3PM with Mr. Tollerson. He had emailed her congratulating her last night and scheduled a phone briefing for today. She knew he would want to know how soon to expect her back in Boston and she wasn't sure she wanted to return.

She wasn't missing the city. Not really. She missed the holiday lights and events she was usually too busy to attend, but she wasn't in a rush to get back like she thought she would be by now. She missed Darcy's cat, Cuddles, who was now staying with a co-worker of Darcy's until her return from her wedding-moon, but she was content being in Fair Bend. She hadn't expected to feel sad about leaving.

Chapter Twenty

Kara was struggling to wrangle the boys and their carry-on bags as they appeared into view at the airport. Lacey saw the twins rushing towards her and she knelt down onto the floor as they reached her for a double trouble hug. She kissed them both on the cheek and squeezed them tightly almost falling backward. "Hey sis! Oh my gosh, we're finally here. You wouldn't believe the drama," Kara said dropping bags to the floor. "Boys, pick up your bags. You're seven. You can carry your own stuff." She hugged Lacey and muttered in her ear "Mommy needs vodka." Lacey burst into laughter at her sister's obvious stress induced joke. At least, she assumed it was a joke.

"We've got something for the stress at the house, I'm sure. Let's head to baggage claim and you can fill me in on the ride to Romelle's. I've got to make a quick stop to pick up some items from the office I was using there." "Oh, yeah, how are things with work? Never mind, you can fill me in on the ride home. I'm so ready to get these wild ones to the grandparents for some outdoor romping and ridding of all this pent up energy from the three hour flight from Denver. Three hours feels like six with kids. I'm sure I look like I've been hit by a bus. I have been up all night. Ted kept snoring and waking me up as I was barely able to sleep anyway with my nerves ahead of travel. I was up at 3 to get a shower and get the boys up. I had them bathe before bed and Ted took us to the airport to see us off."

The ride to Romelle's was filled with chatter and laughs as Kara rambled on about Ted not filling the car with gas the day before so they had to stop at 5 AM at a convenience store, and how the boys argued on the plane about which movie to watch on the iPad that she had them share with each kid having one earbud in. Lacey didn't envy her having to travel alone with the boys, who were every bit as rambunctious as any seven year old and then of course, there were two of them. After they made their stop by Romelle's, they drove back to Fair Bend. Veronica Myers was standing by the door waving as they pulled up the driveway and honked the horn of the Lexus SUV. The boys ran to their grandmother for a hug and she whisked them inside for hot cocoa and banana bread. She didn't waste any time spoiling her grandchildren.

Kara and Lacey decided to ride into town for a little sisterly bonding to get mani/pedis. They stopped by to see their dad at the hardware store and then headed to The Bend. They were having a much needed therapy session with each other taking turns discussing their stresses. They went by Java House first and as they walked out to go to the nail spa, they passed Millicent. She gave a fake smile and kept going into the coffee shop. "Who was that?" asked Kara noticing the forced smiles between the ladies. "Millie Jenkins. I doubt you remember her. She graduated a year behind me, and was always the town—well, you know. She was kind of a *loosey goosey* as mom would say." The two laughed at their mother's corny southern-isms.

"I think she went out with Mason a few times recently, and she saw us talking here one day. She kind of gave him a hard time about it thinking we were together. I don't know. She's always been a drama queen, but I don't pay her any mind. Mason said she was talking to some other guy in the parking lot right after she gave him the quiz about us, so I'm not sure why she is so snide towards me. It's not like she and Mason were in a relationship and I came into town and ruined it. She doesn't like anyone that she thinks stands between her and the man of the month. She'll be smirking at someone else next month."

Lacey was not going to be bothered by the petty childish ways of Millicent. She was the least of her concerns. "I'm more interested in the fact that you have seen Mason since you've been home. Do tell. Was it just once or have you been hanging out with him?" Kara inquisitively stared at her sister. *Here we go.* Lacey knew she had to fill her in on the one topic she was avoiding. Mason Peters. "It's a good thing we're going to be here for a while and that I don't recognize anyone so I can speak freely, because this may take a while." Lacey opened up to her sister and shared her renewed feelings that were only becoming stronger for Mason as she tried keeping her distance.

"I thought I could see him and be nonchalant and easy breezy, you know. We'd say our hellos and maybe I'd run into him once or twice. I didn't expect him to actually want to spend time with me. It threw me for a loop and I guess I just rolled with it. At first, I didn't think much about it. We went to Java House and talked about this and that. Random stuff.

Then, after the night we went to see the play in Charlotte, things started to feel more like the old days, I mean sort of. Different but the same."

"Mom told me you had gone with him to see A Christmas Carol. She told me to act like I didn't know anything about it, but she knew then you were falling for Mason again. She watched you from the window downstairs talking and she said for a moment it seemed like she was looking at you two in high school again at the end of a date," Kara admitted as she touched her sister's hand. "I know you've never really let anyone else in."

Lacey felt a knot forming in her stomach. "I

wrestled with whether to go over to his house or not more times than I care to recall, but I couldn't stay away. I went to his house for dinner, and when things got heated, I panicked. I basically left within five minutes like a crazy person. I'm sure he thought so. I mean, he hasn't called or texted me, so I'm pretty certain he has chosen to just throw whatever feelings he was having out the window as a temporary lapse in judgment."

"This pedicure is just what I need. I don't want to think about Mason Peters. I want to relax and spend some much needed time with you. I've missed you so much, sis." Lacey took a sip of the hibiscus tea she and Kara had gotten from the coffee shop and sighed. "Happy thoughts. No more Mason talk. What's new with you besides the headache of getting here today." In typical fashion, Lacey deflected to a new topic.

"I know what you're doing, Lacey. I will bring this back up later tonight, but for now, I'll let it go with this one comment. Mason was heartbroken when you left. I think he married that girl on a whim to try and get over you, but I don't think he would've stayed with her for very long even if she hadn't been the one to leave. I also have a secret. I never told you because I didn't want to make it harder on you in Boston or have you regret your choices.

His cousin, Marianne, you know she and I were

123

good friends in school. Well, we keep in touch and I saw her when I was home visiting about a year after you left. She told me Mason had thrown himself into work, but the family knew he was devastated when you moved away. She said he admitted he bought a train ticket and was all set to surprise you, which he knew could've been a mistake, but his grandfather passed. He never mentioned going after that."

Lacey was speechless. She sipped her tea and looked out the spa windows at passers-by shopping and smiling. *He was going to come to Boston. He bought a train ticket?* She didn't even know how to process that.

She was interrupted from her thoughts to move to the table for her manicure and a text from Mr. Tollerson's assistant reminding her of their scheduled phone call in two hours.

Chapter Twenty-One

Mason was putting tools in his bag and preparing to leave the municipal complex where he was working when Millicent walked by the room he was working in. "Oh, hi Mason. I didn't realize you were on site. Should we all be concerned if an electrician is in the building?" She was bubbly and acting as if she hadn't lectured him the last time she'd seen him about blowing her off. He preferred if she didn't rehash any drama and if he could get away from her unscathed. "No worries. Just an annual inspection requirement. I'll be on my way now" he said in an effort to get past her as she stood in the doorway.

She stepped in front of him and cut him off. "I wanted to thank you, Mason." "Thank me? Umm. OK. You're welcome. I really have to get going." Mason was in no mood to get pulled into some psycho babble mind game. Millicent giggled with a laugh that sounded like a witch about to cast a spell. "You do make me laugh, Mason Peters. I wanted to thank you for standing me up for my office holiday party." Mason didn't stand her up; he canceled, but didn't want to give her reason to debate and keep him there further, so he continued listening with a blank stare. "Anyway, I met the most devilishly gorgeous man, but I didn't think he was interested. I have no idea why I thought he wasn't, but I digress. About a week ago, his mother, who works in the office upstairs, came down and asked for my number and the rest is..well, too juicy to tell." "That's good to hear, Millie. I'm glad you are happy. Now, I really must-- "I know, I know. You're in such a hurry. Busy man, you are. I just wanted to thank you for doing me a favor and I'm sorry things with Lacey didn't work out. I guess you can't compete with hunky city slickers. But don't worry. There are plenty of fish in the sea, right? Oh that's right, you insisted you two were only friends anyway, so I guess I see now that I overreacted. She looked smitten with her beau in Charlotte last night all cozied up at a fancy romantic bistro."

Millicent was pleased with herself as she saw Mason's face harden and his brows furrow. He tried to act unaffected, but he was crushed. Maybe that's why Lacey pulled away and rushed out the other night. She had someone in Boston coming down to see her in Charlotte and didn't want to tell him. She was probably hoping to avoid hurting him. Why did she even come over then? A myriad of questions burned on his mind as he walked out of the complex ignoring Millicent as she apologized insincerely for upsetting him. "I'm sorry. I thought you knew" she sneered.

Mason didn't know what to think. He decided it

was best to leave it alone. He was glad Millicent had told him, although he wished Lacey had been honest with him if there were someone else. He had planned on calling her that night after giving her some space. It was best that Millicent had told him about seeing her so he wouldn't waste his time professing love for someone who had apparently forgotten about him a long time ago. He continued to replay their encounters of the past few weeks. *She must have had a momentary weakness the other night. Just old feelings stirred up from seeing me but nothing that would change anything from the way it is. Her in Boston. Me in Fair Bend. Nothing to fight for.*

She obviously knows I still care for her. I love her. She may know that, too. If she still loved me, she wouldn't be spending time with someone else. She wouldn't have rushed away from me so quickly the other night. Mason decided to keep his feelings for Lacey to himself and let her go once and for all.

Chapter Twenty-Two

Lacey completed her call with Mr. Tollerson and walked into the foyer where her mom and sister were decorating the sparkle tree the three of them had decorated when they were younger. The same beautiful ornaments in pink, blue, purple, and silver were as lovely as she remembered. "We're ready when you are. I thought this would be a good year to add the sparkle tree again since both of my girls are home. The boys were tired from playing board games with me and baking gingerbread cookies, so they are napping. That long flight wore them out." Veronica put an arm around each daughter's shoulder and squeezed them. "We'd love to decorate the sparkle tree, mom" Kara said kissing her mother on the cheek. Lacey followed suit and kissed her other cheek.

After they were done with the tree, they sat at the table for a gingerbread cookie and coffee. Rick came in bringing in firewood for the fireplace from the wood box on the deck. "Hey there my beautiful ladies! Where are my grand kids?" "Upstairs taking a nap" Veronica replied as she offered him a bite of her cookie. Kara gave her dad a hug. Lacey walked over to pour her dad a cup of coffee and noticed the wood box. "Dad, where did you get that wood box? I haven't even noticed it until now, although I've only been on the deck a couple of times since I've been home. I've seen it I suppose, but have never really noticed it's design. It's very sturdy, but what I like is the colors of the wood. It looks like something Mason would create." Lacey smiled at the thought of Mason's creativity and joy he had found in crafting furniture from wood. "It looks like something Mason would create because Mason did create it. He made it for me back in the summer. He delivered it Thanksgiving weekend. He's pretty darn talented. That's a good man. I hate you two didn't work out." Lacey gave a nod and a forced smile as she walked back over to her seat at the table.

"I have news. I wanted to wait until dad got home. I spoke with my boss about an hour ago and he offered me a promotion. The one I've been waiting for. The one I've been busting my butt for. VP of Romelle's. An offer to design my own line for the store was not immediately on the table, but he mentioned it was something to be discussed when I return to Boston. A huge salary increase, as well." Lacey shared her news realizing she wasn't sounding nearly as happy as she thought she would. She should be ecstatic but instead she felt rather lackluster. She felt proud, but she didn't feel the excitement she had anticipated a few weeks ago.

"That's wonderful, honey," Veronica praised as

she noticed the half-hearted enthusiasm coming from her younger daughter. "Why don't you seem more excited about it? I thought this is what you wanted?" "It is. It was. I don't know. I've just got so much on my mind. I haven't mentioned it, but you know I've been meeting with Alexia Dodson and creating a new design space for a few rooms in her home in case they put it on the market." "You mean, you aren't still calling her by all three names?" Veronica quipped. "You were right in saying there was more going on under the surface with her. Her husband is not the perfect husband by any means. I think she may be headed for a divorce, although she hasn't said that. He's been in California for a few months and she said he isn't coming home for Christmas as planned now. It seems like they are definitely in a rocky place. Anyway, she offered to help me with referrals if I were to consider opening my own design firm. I didn't give it much thought at first, but over the last week, it's kind of been in the back of my mind."

Lacey continued. "I have felt a newfound passion for design by working with her and am feeling invested personally in what I've been doing in creating ideas for her. It makes me feel like I'm helping her take back some control in her life and make other positive changes from the alterations she's making to her home. I know that sounds over the top, but it's true. I feel empowered when I design something as simple as a pillow cover. I'm skilled at what I do for Romelle's. I can close the deals. I get the best products for the lowest prices. What I select for the departments I purchase for bring in solid sales. That pleases me and makes me feel accomplished, but doesn't invigorate me. I'm starting to wonder if I should chart a new course and perhaps give my own design studio a chance. It was my original dream, after all. It took Alexia of all people to remind me of that."

Lacey's family exchanged looks and sat quietly absorbing this revelation. Kara was the first to speak. "Well, I think it would be fabulous for you to go out on your own. You have dedicated ten years to Romelle's. You've learned so much about the market and what sells and what doesn't. You've always had an eye for design." Veronica added "We support you either way. I don't know much about design and business or even your job for that matter, but I do know my children. You would be successful at anything you set your mind to. You've proven that."

Rick concluded "If you decide to make a change, you know we're behind you. You know I own the whole building that the hardware store is in and the renters who have had the space next to me are moving out in a few weeks. I would give you the space for free for six months and then we can work out an affordable rent if you're getting on your feet."

"I am just thinking out loud. I haven't made any decisions. I'm likely going to go back to

Boston and think it over. My lease ends in late January and with Darcy being on her wedding-moon, I may move into a new apartment if I stay in Boston anyway. It's a lot to consider. I don't want to make a hasty decision about anything. I may open the design studio in Boston. I could do it on the side in my extremely rare free time, that is.

I could also resign from Romelle's and take a chance and open a design firm there. It would be easier here in some ways, but likely more lucrative there in the long run. Let's table the conversation for now. Christmas Eve is in two days and I will be leaving soon either way, at least temporarily, so let's enjoy the time together and celebrate."

They did just that. The rest of the evening was filled with laughs; playing games and watching Rudolph and Frosty with the twins on television.

Chapter Twenty-Three

Christmas Eve..........

Ted and Rick took the boys to the hardware store for a coat drive Rick held every holiday continuing the tradition that the former owner had started many years earlier when Rick worked for him. The ladies stopped by and dropped off donations Lacey had purchased from Romelle's her last day on-site. It was heartwarming to see the people of Fair Bend giving during the season and spreading holiday cheer. Lacey was honored to be her father's daughter. She and Kara posed with their parents, Ted & the boys for a photo for the newspaper.

Lacey and Kara checked out the space that would soon be available on the other side of the building. It was perfect for her studio vision. Exposed brick interior with wall panels that were ideal for hanging artwork and metal items. She couldn't help but consider the possibilities of it all.

As Lacey and Kara exited the building, they saw Mason walking away from one of the coat drop off bins. "Go say something to him" Kara insisted nudging Lacey's arm. "Here's your chance. Tell him how you feel. You're not calling or showing up at his house. You're in the same place at the same time. It would be rude not to acknowledge him." "Not if he doesn't see me. I don't know what to say. He doesn't want to talk to me. I haven't heard from him all week." "He hasn't heard from you either, has he?" Kara asserted.

Lacey anxiously approached Mason and as he noticed her walking toward him, he stopped. Hands in his pockets, his signature move when he felt uncomfortable, he took a deep breath as she neared. "Hi, Mason." "Hey." The two stood there for a moment; neither sure of what to say next. Lacey broke the silence. "I just wanted to wish you a Merry Christmas. You, and your family." "Same to you, Lacey. This is a nice event your dad does. Good of him to continue that tradition." Silence resumed. After a few moments of glances at each other and then averting to other directions, Mason spoke. "Look. I wanted to call you. I know things got a little weird. We said some things that needed to be said. It's natural that old feelings would come into play when rehashing the past."

Mason seemed so calm although he still was shifting his body and keeping his hands in his pocket. Lacey knew he was keeping his feelings inside, but she assumed he had his reasons and had made the choice not to pursue anything further with her.

"I want you to know that I will always care about you, Mason. Always. I just wanted to say that before I leave. I am headed back to Boston in a few days. I was offered the promotion I had been hoping for."

"That's great news Lacey. I have never had any doubt that you'd be successful at any endeavor you pursue. I wish you nothing but the best." After a moment, he continued "I hope you have a safe trip back to Boston. Will your boyfriend be staying with you for Christmas or did he head back already? Never mind. That's none of my business. See ya Lacey."

"My boyfriend? What are you talking about? What boyfriend?" Lacey was flabbergasted. "Millicent said she saw you having dinner with some corporate suit in Charlotte earlier this week. She said you were in a romantic restaurant. I just assumed as she did that someone you're seeing in Boston flew in to see you."

"That was a business dinner. He was a vendor that flew down for a meeting to secure the biggest deal of my career with Romelle's. It was nothing more than that. Why would you listen to Millicent of all people anyway? Why didn't you call and ask me?" Lacey persisted. "I shouldn't have listened to her. I just figured that you left because there was someone else. That was easier to accept than you leaving because you didn't return my feelings. You know I've never been the jealous type." Mason said embarrassed that he had fallen prey to Millicent's deception. He should have known better than to take anything she would say at face value.

"I have a gift for you. I left it with your dad a few minutes ago. He said you were here, but he wasn't sure if you had left on a coffee run or something. I just wanted to get it to you before you left for Boston. It's in the back on Rick's desk." "Mason, you shouldn't have. I was going to get a gift for you, but I didn't think I'd see you again before leaving. I didn't want to make things more complicated. I thought it would be best if I just went back to Boston and took some time to think over possibilities with my career."

Mason's curiosity was peeked. "I know you mentioned you were considering a change, but I didn't know you were serious about opening a design firm here. Is that something you want? I didn't say anything when you brought it up at dinner because I didn't want you to feel like I was trying to influence your decisions. I would never do that."

"I know you wouldn't. I would have no expectation of being in your life if I did choose to move back, Mason. I guess I should get going. Dad probably needs me to help out with the coats. Thank you for the gift in advance.

That was thoughtful of you." They turned and walked away stopping to look back and smile at each other.

Lacey found the gift on the desk. It was a handcrafted wooden canister with Lacey's Java carved into it. Inside was a bag of coffee beans waiting to be ground and poured inside. Kara walked up as Lacey rubbed her fingers across the lettering. "He knows you well" Kara remarked putting her hands on her sister's shoulders and peering around her. "It's lovely, isn't it? He's so talented. I just adore it. Kara, how do I walk away from him again? I don't know if I can do it this time." She turned to her sister and Kara hugged her. Lacey began to cry.

After a few minutes, she regained her composure and they joined her parents to finish up the coat drive. She had much to consider.

Chapter Twenty-Four

Christmas Day.....

Laughter, hugs, wrapping paper, bows, gift bags, and love were abound in the Myers' household. Friends and neighbors had stopped by over the course of the past two days with homemade goodies. It really was magical being surrounded by everyone she loved; almost everyone, that is.

That night, as things quieted down and the family activities settled, Lacey continued a project from the night before. She resumed sewing a large pillow cover made of burlap with small flannel squares after picking up the supplies on Christmas Eve and was working in her mother's sewing room as the boys played with toys and the rest of the family watched "It's a Wonderful Life." She completed the pillow and stitched Zeke across the top and a bone underneath. She then made a throw pillow with the same fabrics but no wording and on the back, she stitched in small lettering, *All My Love, L.M.*

She planned to take the gifts to Mason the next day. She would be leaving the day after.

Her mother walked in and sat down beside her. "Lacey, those pillows are wonderful. She picked up the throw pillow and looked at the back. She tearfully put it down and stood up. You know, you could let your guard down and see what happens. I know you don't want a man to be what guides your choices, but that doesn't mean one can't be an added perk to a particular choice. You'll make the best decision, I have no doubt, but maybe a path that follows your heart this time may be the one that makes all of your dreams come true. Sometimes, we fly away never to return and sometimes, we go home again and that's OK too." Veronica pointed to the pillow's stitching. You're talented and can do anything you set your mind to, L M." She kissed her daughter on the head and closed the door.

Chapter Twenty-Five

Lacey drove up the winding driveway to Mason's home. She was greeted by Zeke and almost fell to the ground when he snuggled up to her with full force and started licking her hand. "I have something for you, big guy. She handed him a treat from a bag she had purchased on the way.

Mason wasn't home. His grandfather's old truck was unlocked. She noticed fishing rods and a tackle box in the back. He must drive it when he goes fishing. She remembered he used to love going fishing with his grandfather and father growing up. She left the gifts inside and a note on the door to the house. She had prepared in case he wasn't home. The note read:

Mason,

I hope your Christmas has been special. I love my coffee canister and can't wait to use it. I hope you and Zeke will enjoy these pillows. I am leaving for Boston in the morning. I am still debating on whether to return to Fair Bend or stay in Boston. Either way, I have decided to turn down the position with Romelle's and venture out on my own. It's a scary step, but I have the greatest support system in my family and friends. You were the one who told me in high school that I should be an interior designer when I kept making over everyone's bedroom. You inspired me then, and you've inspired me now. You are talented and you aren't letting your talent go to waste.

I hope you continue to do what gives you joy. I want to feel that euphoric feeling again. Kara told me you once had a train ticket to Boston, but never told me. Here is a plane ticket. If you aren't busy for New Year's Eve, maybe you will use it. If not, just know that your feelings were returned. Just read the back of your pillow.

Love,
Lacey

P.S. My address is on the back of this note, although you've always had the directions to my heart.

Chapter Twenty-Six

December 29th......

Lacey had been back in Boston for two days and had officially turned in her resignation with a guarantee to stay through January during the set up of the spring line she had helped land with Alberson's. She had sent emails to vendors assuring them she would aid in a smooth transition and her decision to leave was to pursue her own design agency. She felt anxious yet exhilarated thinking of her new venture.

She took off the afternoon early and went to her favorite spots around Beacon Street and towards Beacon Hill. She had fallen in love with Boston on her first visit as soon as she took her first few steps on Beacon. The turn-of-the-century buildings, the Boston Public Garden, the cobble stone street on Acorn, the museums, and taverns. She would miss this beautiful city. Yet, a yearning in her heart beckoned to her southern country roots again. The horses, the mountains in view, rolling hills —wide open spaces. She would spend much time in Charlotte and still partake in cultural arts and yoga. She would make more time for herself and those close to her heart. She would find the balance between career and living life.

She stopped her stroll to answer her phone. She sat on an empty park bench and answered as the cold wind was starting to set in. This would be a short walk. "Hi, Alexia. How are you?" "I won't keep you but a sec. I'm on the way to teach a cardio class at the clubhouse with some of the ladies in my neighborhood. Anyhoo, just wanted to say, we've decided to stay in Charlotte, but I still want to do the redecorating. Just maybe tweak a few things since we're going to be here instead of appealing to the masses. Still, you're absolutely right about my house being too stuffy. I do want to have a more relaxed feel, but just a little." "Sounds good, Alexia. So, what happened with your husband? Did he come home for Christmas after all or is he still in California?" Lacey asked cautiously.

"He's here. I gave him a piece of my mind and an ultimatum. Honestly, I wasn't sure how it was all going to go, but I was sticking to my guns either way. He is going to open a practice here, but only open four days a week and we're going next weekend to check out a few properties in Hilton Head. I compromised. He wants golf. I want the beach. We both want warmer temperatures, so most of the year, we can still have those things without moving to the opposite side of the country. We just won't have it all the time. Brinkley wants to stay here near his school and his friends. He has made a good friend at the children's center in his karate class. I'm so happy for him. So, anyway, I've gotta run. I have three ladies dying to meet with you and get design plans underway. Tell me you're coming back? I know you've decided to give your own agency a go, but I do hope you'll consider doing it in North Carolina." Alexia was nothing if not persistent.

"Yes, Alexia. I will be moving back in the end of January. I'm looking forward to working with you and the clients you send my way. Your house will be free of my service charge for the many referrals I expect you to bring in." "Ciao, doll." She hung up before Lacey could respond.

Chapter Twenty-Seven

New Year's Eve.....

Lacey hadn't heard from Mason since leaving
Fair Bend, other than a text message simply
stating *thanks for the pillows. Zeke is already
enjoying his. Talk soon. Be safe driving back.*
Nothing more. She had responded *I will and
you're welcome.* She opened her heart for the
first time truly since she left Mason all those
years ago, but she knew she had once crushed
his heart. She understood if he didn't want to
take a chance on her again. Maybe if she moved
back to Fair Bend, something would happen.
Maybe not. At least, she had taken the chance.
She had followed Darcy's advice to live in the
moment and not over-analyze every decision,
albeit possibly too late as far as matters of the
heart. At least, she was putting that advice to
good use in her career. She had decided to
move back to Fair Bend and utilize the six
months rent-free space at her father's
commercial building to get started.

She called Darcy to congratulate she and Mark
on their wedding day, as it was an hour ahead

in Aruba and the wedding should commence in two hours. "Well, hello soon-to-be Mrs. Keisley!" Lacey said as she held her phone in front of her already expecting a shriek from her friend. "Eeeek! It is almost that time, isn't it? I'm hoping I will be dressed in time. I think I've eaten too much this week and now I'm trying to force myself into my dress," Darcy lamented. "I'm sure that will not be an issue," Lacey reassured jokingly. "So, give me the scoop. Unfortunately, it will have to be the abbreviated version for now as I am in a race against showtime, but I want all the deets upon my return," Darcy directed as Lacey could hear her knocking something over in the background and beginning to sound slightly out of breath. "Are you OK?" "Yes, go on. I'm not bleeding, so it's all good." They both giggled.

"Abbreviated version is this. I turned down the promotion and tendered my resignation to Mr. Tollerson this week. I've decided to follow my passion and open my own interior design agency and continue designing pieces under my business name; *Pillows and Lace Designs*. That will also be the agency name." "Lacey, that's wonderful! I'm so excited for you! How thrilling, babe!" "Thanks so much. I have also got some not so happy news. I've chosen to move back to Fair Bend, as my dad offered me a space for free while I'm getting the start-up off the ground. It's spacious and ideal for both the agency and for a design area."

"I will miss you to pieces, but of course you will visit and I will visit you, as well, as naturally I will hire you to redecorate the man cave Mark currently has in place in our townhouse," Darcy added. "One more burning question. You know what or shall I say whom the question is about." After a moment of pause, Lacey replied "Jury's still out on that one, but it doesn't look like I'm going to hear from him. I left a gift for Mason and one for his dog, Zeke, with a note asking him to join me for New Year's Eve. I had hoped he would respond, but so far, not a word." "He will be in touch. Lacey. Mason loves you. He'd be a fool to miss out on the best woman in the world. Feel free to tell him I said that or I'll tell him personally if you'd like." "Calm down. Don't get your panties in a bunch over my love life on your wedding day. Whatever will be will be. Like you said. I'm going to take it one day at a time. I reached out. I understand if he chooses not to pursue more than friendship. I have never made it easy to be with me." Lacey was hoping to hide her disappointment as she truly did want to let fate take over and see where it may lead for a change.

As their conversation ended, Lacey thought about the first time she met Darcy. She would miss her friend. This would not be goodbye. It wouldn't be farewell to Boston either, but it no longer felt like home. Fair Bend was home. She was missing being there already.

She decided to put on a dress and heels and ring in the new year rather than feeling depressed about Mason. She had made plans to join a few friends at an event with hors d'oeuvres, cocktails, and jazz. She paused for a moment to sit by the living room window noticing snowflakes falling upon the fogged pane. It was already becoming a blanket of white under the spectacle of illumination of Brighton. The street lights intermixed with Christmas lights that were still twinkling from across the way in neighboring apartments. As she was about to leave, there was a knock at her door. She peered into the peephole to see Mason on the other side. She opened the door and there he stood, wearing a black leather coat, and purposely messy hair. He was damp and wiping his jacket as he wasn't quite prepared for winter in Boston.

"Am I too late? I landed just as the snow began. It took me longer than expected to get here. I guess in more ways than one, you could say. You look beautiful." "You're right on time. Why didn't you tell me you were coming, though?" "And ruin the surprise? Where's the fun in that? I was just hoping I wouldn't get here to find you already gone out. I was taking a risk, believe me, I know. This could've gone all wrong." He smiled his twisted warm smile that won Lacey's heart all those years ago, again when she first saw him by the fountain a few weeks ago, and right now. "Lace, I know ten years have come and gone and we aren't two teenagers or college kids anymore. I am not here with expectation. I read your note three times. I don't want to watch you walk away again without letting you know how much I love you. I've loved for you since we were seventeen; even before then. If Boston is where you need to be, if you want me, if you really want me in your life, then Boston will have to be my home, as well. I won't let you go so easily this time." Lacey wrapped her arms around Mason as he wiped a tear from her cheek, and held her closely while pulling her lips to his.

"I've decided to move back to Fair Bend at the end of January," Lacey said as they pulled out of their heated kiss. "Thank God. I really didn't want to move. Zeke definitely didn't want to move. I love our little town, but not as much as I love you, Lacey Myers." "I love you with all of my heart and soul, Mason Peters. Thank you for giving me the chance to find my way back to you again, without pressure, and with patience. You are my soul mate. You're the one no one could measure up to and I have let very few even try. Thank you for giving me space when I needed it all those years ago to fly. My wings led me home again, where my heart has always been. With you."

They joined her friends and celebrated the end of one year and the start of the next. They danced close, kept their eyes peeled on each other, and toasted champagne to the new year.

"Happy New Year, Lacey." "Happy New Year, Mason." As confetti poured from every direction encompassing them in their embrace, Mason lifted Lacey up over his shoulders and spun her around gently gliding her back into his arms as she beamed and laughed. They began dancing slowly again as the band performed an instrumental version of Auld Lang Syne. The sparkle of champagne and glitter paled in comparison to that of Lacey and Mason. It may have taken a winding road of bumps and curves to get here, but they were here, nevertheless.

THE END

Epilogue:
Christmas in Fair Bend

A Moonlit Hearts Romance

Angie Ellington

© 2017

One year later......

"Today's the day. The day our paths join as one. I can't wait to see you standing at the front of the church waiting for me." Mason felt his eyes welling up with tears as he read the note Lacey had left for him on the kitchen table alongside a hand-sewn handkerchief with their wedding date stitched along the bottom. Lacey had used her key to slip in early that morning while she knew Mason would be taking Zeke for a ride in his grandfather's pick-up truck. He could hardly wait to make her his bride. It had been his only unfulfilled dream for as long as he could remember.

Lacey's mother entered the room in the back of the old white country church typically used for Sunday school lessons with the children, and the same room Lacey and Kara had spent their childhood attending. "This moment seems surreal. I feel like it should have happened and that this is almost deja vu in a way. In my mind, you have always been destined to marry Mason, and I think somewhere inside, I held on to the hope that someday you'd return home to Fair Bend, even it was just to reclaim your love. Your father and I couldn't be more proud of all that you've accomplished, and now, we celebrate our younger daughter's wedding day, with literal icing on the cake!" Veronica Myers gently wiped her daughter's hair back from her brow and tucked it inside her veil. "How do I look?" Lacey asked as she viewed her reflection in the full length mirror she had ordered for her design studio from Mason. It was a deep cherry wood with an easy roller set attached to the bottom allowing for lighter ease of transporting from room to room. Lacey insisted Kara bring it to the church and as she took a deep breath, she placed her hand along the wooden etching at the top of the mirror and smiled.

Kara entered the room, almost frantically. "It's time! Are you ready, Lacey? Let's get this show on the road, sis! I have two boys fighting over the rings on the pillow already. I told them if they didn't stop, I would make one of them carry the flowers." Lacey turned to face her older sibling. "Oh, gosh, Lacey. You look stunning!" Lacey hugged her mother and sister as they prepared to walk to the outside of the church doors. "Kara, we do still have an actual flower girl, right?," Lacey inquired with a bit of concern. "Yes, of course. Mason's cousin's little girl would throw a total tantrum in the middle of the aisle if someone tried to take that basket out of her tiny hands. The boys are older, so they are walking right behind her to make sure she doesn't veer off when she sees her mother." The ladies laughed heartily as the photographer appeared taking the first shots. "I apologize that I didn't make it back to the room after your mother arrived for more images, but I was delayed with the groom's family. We will get plenty after the ceremony." "It's fine. We wanted some time alone, anyway," Lacey reassured.

Just as Lacey's mother and sister entered the church, Lacey heard a voice coming from behind her. "Lacey, oh geez, Lacey, I'm so sorry. I got stuck in stupid traffic in Charlotte after the Christmas parade!" It was

Alexia. Lacey was not too surprised she was late. At least she made it before Lacey started down the aisle, although that wouldn't have been unlike Alexia to draw a little spotlight to herself during someone else's moment. Lacey shook her head and smiled. "Get inside, woman!"

Moments later, as the music played and the crowd of family and friends rose and turned to watch the bride, Lacey entered the church in an elegant lace and silk gown that was simple and timeless. It was fitted to the waist and draped loosely to her ankles. She carried a bouquet of simple red roses and greenery. Perfect for a Christmas wedding. Kara and Darcy, along with Mason's dad and his cousin, Tim, stood next to them. It was a beautiful ceremony, with simple vows, and longing looks of bliss.

As sunset began to fade over Fair Bend, Lacey and Mason danced the first dance to Michael Buble's "Save the Last Dance for Me" as the guests joined in, and began cheering them along for a kiss. Mason obliged their requests with a dip and kiss followed by a spin back into his arms. They left the church in Mason's grandfather's old green Ford F-1 pickup with a red bow on the front and battery-operated lights entwined around the wooden rails he had added to the back.

Indeed, it was a Christmas to remember for everyone in Fair Bend that year, as Lacey and Mason began their lives together as one. As he carried her over the threshold into their home, Zeke barked and ran in behind them tugging at Mason's leg. "Zeke, get outside boy!" Mason ordered unable to hold back laughter. "No, let him come in with us. I wouldn't have this day any other way. I love you so much, Mr. Peters," Lacey said as she kissed Mason on the cheek and squeezed his neck. "I love you for now and always, Mrs. Peters," Mason replied kicking the door shut behind him with his foot. "Merry Christmas, baby," he whispered as he kissed her on the forehead after gently lowering her to her feet. Just as they turned toward the window, they saw a shooting star. "No need for wishes tonight," Lacey said taking Mason's hand. "We've got everything. Well, maybe one wish is left." They smiled and locked the door.

THE END

Author Bio

Angie Ellington is a novelist from NC.

She enjoys writing contemporary women's fiction and romance. To find out about future book releases, visit www.angienellington.com

75614082R00087

Made in the USA
Columbia, SC
18 September 2019